TEXAS

COWBOYS & CAMPFIRES

To Jean –
Happy trails!
Nancy Alana

Nancy Sifford Alana

ISBN: 1493553577
ISBN 13: 9781493553570
Library of Congress Control Number: 2013920052
CreateSpace Independent Publishing Platform
North Charleston, South Carolina

St. Augustine, Texas, Jan'y 9, 1836

I expect in all probability to settle on the Bodark or Choctaw Bayou of Red River. That, I have no doubt, is the richest country in the world. Good Land and plenty of timber, and the best springs and good mill streams. Good range, clear water and ever appearance of good health, and game plenty. It is in the pass where the Buffalo passes from the north to south and back twice a year, and bees and honey plenty. - David Crockett

David Crockett died 57 days later at the Alamo on March 6, 1836.

Dedicated to my city slickers:
Jacob, Dylan, and Heston

Acknowledgements

I would like to thank these people
who have inspired me and helped me with this book:
Kenneth Hendricks– Great-Great-Grandson of David and
Elizabeth Crockett
Kellie Dilka Lambert – Miss Rodeo America, 1988
Donald H. Alana
Jacob, Dylan, and Heston Alana
Averie Coffman
Janie Green
Dixie Lee Hedgecock
Rebecca Lucas
Laine Meek
Margaret Whitt Sifford
Bob and Jo Ann Skelton
Sharon Williams

Table of Contents

CHAPTER 1
SUMMER BEGINS

HANK combed through the thick green grass in the neighborhood park. He wasn't aware of the fluffy white clouds floating in the beautiful blue sky or the singing cicadas in the tall trees towering over his head. He was looking intently for anything that moved in the grass that he could put into his bug cage. So far his only options were ants, small beetles, and roly poly bugs. He finally looked up from the ground and saw his older brothers on their way home.

Hank's brothers, Justin and Dallas, laughed when they looked back at their little brother trying to catch some sort of critter to take home. He always managed to find something to put in his cage, but today it seemed he was out of luck. The last time he went out looking for a critter for his bug cage, he found a small garden snake, but he had to look under some rocks before he found it. Today, they didn't have time to look under any rocks.

"Come on, Hank," said Justin. "It's time to go home."

Justin was the oldest of the brothers. He was ten years old, smart, and a good leader. He had black hair that was thick and straight. Under all that hair, he had a great mind with an ever-active imagination that took him to all sorts of places doing all sorts of things. Life was never boring for Justin. All he needed was a good book, an electronic game, or his Pokémon cards, and he could immediately be transformed to another time and place. Justin was able to tell you facts about many things he had studied or read about, but he especially knew a lot about sharks. He was already looking forward to a career as a marine biologist.

Dallas was nine years old. He and Justin were close enough in age that it sometimes seemed as if they were twins, but they didn't look anything alike. Dallas was a little shorter than Justin, had curly brown hair, and wore glasses. He was as quick as lightning when he ran. He was smart, creative, and very sensitive to the needs of others. He was the first one to jump in and help anyone who needed it.

Then, there was Hank. He tried hard to keep up with his big brothers wherever they went. He was just beginning to learn about the world, but he already knew he liked sports. He could sit and watch football or baseball on television for a long time with his dad. He had quite a large collection of baseballs, footballs, soccer balls, and basketballs in his room. Hank also loved to explore the great outdoors especially when he had his big brothers with him. Hank was a happy child and loved the outdoor life.

It was the beginning of June in Texas. Justin, Dallas, and Hank were out of school at last and hoping for an exciting summer. The best thing about summer was the freedom they had to sleep late, play outside, create their own adventures, and visit their grandparents.

Their grandparents lived on a cattle ranch in Hood County, Texas. The ranch had enough cattle and horses to keep the ranch going as a business. The cows produced calves and the calves grew up and were sent to market. Then new calves were born, and the process began again.

There was always work to be done on the ranch. Cattle needed to be fed, tagged, doctored, and moved to fresh pastures on a regular schedule. Fences needed to be checked and mended. The horses had to be fed, water, groomed, shoed, and doctored.

The cowboys, or ranch hands, were an absolute necessity on the Double A. They lived on the ranch in the bunkhouse. Ace and Ms. Adaline, the grandparents of the boys, made sure the ranch hands had everything they needed including clean sheets, towels, and enough good food to eat well and do their work every day. And, work hard they did! From sun up to sun down, they worked. Even on Sundays and holidays, the cowboys had work to do, although they tried to get a few hours each week to spend with their families and friends.

The boys could hardly wait to get to the Double A. They enjoyed helping out at the ranch, but mostly they enjoyed meeting the cowboys and listening to their stories. The boys never knew for sure what was true whenever a cowboy started up with a story. The cowboys seemed to have a knack at adding to a story to make it sound bigger and better every time it was told. True or not, the boys enjoyed all of the stories.

Now that summer had arrived, the boys were ready to start packing their boots and cowboy hats to go see their grandparents. This year they planned to stay two weeks and longer if they could find a way. With one more night at home, they crawled into bed for a good night's sleep. Their summer adventure at the Double A Ranch would begin the next day.

CHAPTER 2

Breakfast and Mom's Reminders

HANK was the first one up on the day the boys were scheduled to go to the Double A Ranch. Even though he still had on his Spiderman pajamas, Hank put on his boots and cowboy hat and began running around the bedroom like a cowboy riding a bucking bronco. Justin sat up in bed and shouted, "Hank! What are you doing?"

"I'm trying to get you up so we can hit the road. Come on, you guys, get up!" said Hank as he galloped out of the room and down the stairs.

The boys' mother was in the kitchen preparing breakfast. She knew the boys would need a good breakfast that would stay with them for a while. She got up early and prepared pancakes for her boys. Setting on the table were glasses full of milk and a bottle of syrup waiting for the boys to get to the table and eat.

"Mom, are you driving us to the ranch?" asked Hank.

"No, your dad has taken the day off and is going to take you to the ranch. He wants you to be ready to leave here at nine o'clock. As soon as you finish eating your pancakes, you need to brush your teeth and get ready. I packed your bags last night, but if there is anything special you want to take with you, you need to get it."

"These pancakes sure do taste good, Mom," said Dallas.

"I'm glad you like them, dear," said Mom. "I wonder what you'll have for lunch when you get to the ranch. What is your favorite dish that Ms. Adaline makes for you at the ranch?"

"My favorites are pecan pie topped with a scoop of vanilla ice cream, pumpkin pie, and anything chocolate," said Justin. He could eat an entire meal of nothing but sweets!

"I love it when she makes corn on the cob and barbecue ribs," said Dallas. "Of course, I love Ms. Adaline's desserts, too. All of them!"

Hank was listening to his brothers and trying to figure out what he was going to say. As he finished his last bite of pancakes and swallowed the last gulp of milk, he said, "My favorites are meatballs and spaghetti and brownies with a scoop of vanilla ice cream on the side! I also like Ms. Adaline's chocolate chip cookies, banana pudding, and pumpkin pie!"

"Well, Ms. Adaline's going to be busy if she tries to cook all of your favorites. I hope you boys will use your manners, tell Ms. Adaline how good her cooking is, and then help her clean up the dishes. She will be doing a lot of extra work around the house just to keep up with you boys, so help her out whenever you can."

"Yes, ma'am," they said at the same time, "we will."

"Boys, I mean it now. You've been taught good manners, and I expect you to use them at the Double A. Even those ole cowboys use good manners." Then she began the run-down of all the table manners she expected them to use. "Take your hat off at the table. Don't burp if you can help it. If you do, say 'excuse me.' Chew with your mouth shut. Use your napkin. Take your dishes to the sink after you've been excused from the table."

"Yes, ma'am, we'll be good," said Dallas. "Don't worry, Mom. We won't embarrass you."

"Well, I hope not," said Mom. "I don't want Ms. Adaline thinking I'm raising a bunch of heathens!" She smiled at the boys fully confident they would be fine. She just needed to make sure she was doing her job as their mother and reminding the boys of how they should behave. "One more thing while I'm thinking about it. Pick up your dirty clothes, and put them in the dirty laundry hamper. Please."

"Hank, be sure and put your Spiderman underwear in the hamper!" teased Justin.

Hank looked at Justin and gave him a fake smile. "I will if you put *your* stinky underwear in the hamper! Phew-eeee!" said Hank as he wrinkled up his nose. Everyone laughed, and the boys put their dishes in the sink. It was time to stop teasing each other and finish getting ready to go.

The boys put on their cowboy gear and looked around the room to see if there was something special they wanted to take with them. Justin decided to take his camera. Dallas picked up a spiral notebook and pencil, and Hank grabbed his binoculars. They were eager to get out the door and on the road.

The boys' dad loaded all the bags into the back of the pickup truck. He looked around to see if he missed anything, gave his wife a peck on the cheek, and climbed into the driver's side. The boys gave their mom a big hug and climbed into the big four-door pickup truck for a two hour ride to the ranch. They would be there just in time for the noon meal with the cowboys. The boys rolled down the windows and waved good-bye to their mom who was standing in the driveway. She waved with one hand and wiped away a tear with the other.

As their mom turned back toward the house, she looked at her beautiful home that was going to be very quiet for the next couple of weeks. However, there was work to be done. The boys did not know that their mom and dad had a surprise to tell them at the end of their visit to the Double A Ranch.

CHAPTER 3
LUNCH AT THE DOUBLE A

THE DOUBLE A RANCH was located in Hood County, Texas. Ace and Ms. Adaline purchased the ranch in 1970. The ranch had 1280 acres of pastures, rocks, creeks, ponds, and a mixture of trees including pecan, mesquite, cedar, juniper, and oak. Over the years, Ace had built several barns, stables, and sheds to fit the needs of the ranch. He and Ms. Adaline had a modest-sized home with three bedrooms known as the Main House. It was the same house that the boys' dad lived in until he graduated from high school and went to school in Lubbock at Texas Tech University. Next to the house was a garage large enough for two vehicles and a tractor. Not far from the house was the bunkhouse for the ranch hands. It had a big open room with bunk beds to sleep about twelve hired-hands. The bunkhouse also had a huge bathroom, a kitchen, and two long tables with benches where the hired-hands ate or played cards.

Since rock was plentiful in Hood County, it made good sense to try to use them however and wherever they could. The rocks were large white rocks and were on top of the ground as well as under the ground. They were heavy to move, but they could be cut or broken into sizes and shapes suitable for building material. Ace used them on his house and the bunkhouse, and he was always trying to figure out how to put it to good use.

"Are we there yet, Dad?" asked Hank. He was keeping an eye out for the entrance to the ranch. The ranch entrance had a big wrought iron sign that had Double A Ranch written on it. On one side of the entrance was an American flag and on the other side was a Texas flag. Since there were lights on the flags at night, the flags stayed posted all the time.

"Almost there, Hank," said Dad. He smiled when he looked in the rear view mirror at Hank. He knew Hank was ready to get out of the pickup and run around. "We'll be there before you can say 'supercalifragilisticexpialidocious.'"

"Before I say what?" asked Hank.

"Supercalifragilisticexpialidocious," said Justin. "Here I'll help you. Say super."

"Super."

"Now say super-cala," said Justin.

"Super-cala," repeated Hank.

"Good," said Justin. "Now say 'super-cala-fragil-istic.'"

"Oh, Justin. It's getting too long," said Hank. Justin gave him a look that said, "Try it!"

"Okay," said Hank. "I'll try. Super-cala-fragil-istic."

"Yes! You said it! Now here is the last part: expe-ala-docious," said Justin. Hank said it back to him correctly. "Now, put it all together: super-cala-fragil-istic-expe-ala-docious."

Hank took a deep breath and said it slowly. "I did it!" said Hank. "Dad, are we there yet?"

"Well, it just so happens I can see the flags flying at the entrance," said Dad.

They pulled up to the ranch about eleven o'clock just in time to get washed up and get out to the bunkhouse for lunch. As soon as their dad parked the pickup, the boys jumped out and ran into the house to see their grandmother. Everyone called her Ms. Adaline, and so the boys did, too. Dallas opened the front door of the Main House and shouted, "Ms. Adaline! We're here!"

Ms. Adaline stuck her head out of the kitchen and said, "Well, get yourself over here, and give me some sugar! I'm just about worn out from walking back and forth to the window to see if you were comin' down the road. My goodness, you boys have grown!" She always said that, and it was true. She loved for the boys to come out to the ranch every summer and get out of the big city and into the fresh country air. She knew what was good for boys, and she made sure they had the chance to explore and learn about the ranch while they were there. And, yes, they *had* grown since she'd last seen them. Kids just have a way of growing up.

Ms. Adaline sent the boys to wash up for lunch. Although Slim was the bunkhouse cook, Ms. Adaline would occasionally cook a meal or two for all the ranch hands. She prepared lunch for them knowing that the grandkids were coming in. She asked them to help her load the food into the Suburban to take down to the bunkhouse. She was ready to go and hoped to get the food out on the counter and ready to serve before the cowboys arrived. If she didn't, she would have to put up with their teasing. They loved Ms. Adaline, and they showed it by teasing her whenever they could.

The boys helped Ms. Adaline load up the Suburban with a big pot of beans, cornbread, roast beef, mashed potatoes, gravy, and a big cooler of sweet tea. She made a big bowl of banana pudding for dessert. Once all the food was loaded up, the boys and their dad jumped in their pickup for the short ride over to the bunkhouse. The dusty road sent out clouds of white dust behind the pickup. The road was rocky and made for a bumpy ride. It reminded the boys of the rides at Six Flags, an amusement park not too far from where they lived in the city.

About the time the food was set out and ready to be served, the door to the bunkhouse flew open, and a big booming voice shouted, "Ms. Adaline, I think we've got some trespassers on our ranch. I saw a bunch of youngin's sneakin' in the front gate." The boys giggled and ran to their grandfather. He was all bark and no bite, and they knew it. He looked like a rough, tough cowboy, talked like a rough, tough cowboy, but he was really just an old softy. He gave each of the boys a hug, threw his cowboy hat on the peg, and went into the kitchen to wash his dirty hands.

Right behind Ace, the other cowboys came into the bunkhouse. As they entered the house, they took off their cowboy hats and placed them on pegs close to the door. They took turns washing up and loading their plates with food. They showered Ms. Adaline with compliments about her food. They appreciated her good food and knew she had been working on it all morning.

The cowboys sat at the two long tables. As soon as everyone was served, Ace said the blessing. When he was finished, everyone said a loud, "Amen!" before they chowed down their lunch.

Ace and Ms. Adaline sat at one end of the table with their son and grandsons. They enjoyed a good conversation with each other and catching up on a few things while they ate. After eating some of Ms. Adaline's banana pudding, the boys' father said good-bye and headed back into the city.

It was time for the fun to begin.

CHAPTER 4
WORKING THE CATTLE

AFTER LUNCH, the cowboys stepped out onto the front porch of the bunkhouse. They used this time every day to report on the work done that morning and create a plan for the afternoon work. Ace said, "Well, boys, what did you managed to get done this morning?"

Rowdy, the ranch foreman spoke for the others. "We moved the cows from the south pasture to the north pasture, and we cut the spring calves from the herd and tagged all of them before it was time to get up here for lunch."

Rowdy was a long, tall cowboy. He had a long moustache, bushy eye brows, and always wore his cowboy boots and hat. He'd been raised on a ranch in South Texas, and he knew exactly what needed to be done without anyone telling him. He'd done all kinds of ranch work over the years from pulling calves when they were born to saying good-bye to the oldest cows and bulls when their work was done. Ace hired him many years ago, and he seemed more like a part of the family than just a ranch hand. Ace was getting to the age that he needed Rowdy to be in charge so he could slow down and take better care of himself.

The boys loved Rowdy as if he were their uncle. He always included them in the work on the ranch and made them feel like they were one of the ranch hands. Every year the boys went home with all kinds of stories to tell their parents and friends about their experiences on the ranch.

"That's good to hear, Rowdy," said Ace. "So, where are you young cowboys headed this afternoon?"

"We thought we'd take these young men across the creek to the far west pasture to see those calves they helped us with last summer. It's time for doctoring up those calves, and we could sure use their help gittin' them down the chute. What do you think, Ace?"

Justin, Dallas, and Hank stood by listening to all this talk with their eyes wide open and moving back and forth between Ace and Rowdy. They couldn't keep the grins off their faces. Ace looked over at the boys, "Well, you boys ready to get started?"

"Yes, sir," they all said at the same time.

"Well, then, let's go. You boys go with Rowdy and the other men while I help Ms. Adaline get these dishes back to the house. I'll try to come out and help you boys later."

Rowdy looked around for his cow dog and whistled. His dog was named Jasper. He was a Border collie with a beautiful black and white coat. Jasper jumped up and ran over to Rowdy with his tail wagging behind him. Rowdy bent down and gave him a good rub down. They were close buddies, and you seldom saw one without the other. Jasper was fed, rested, and eager to go back to work.

The cowboys loaded up in the pickups. Rowdy and four others mounted their horses. Hank, with a little help from one of the cowboys, got on the saddle behind Rowdy. Justin and Dallas shared horses with two other cowboys and rode off toward the west pasture.

To get to the west pasture, the cowboys had to cross a creek. It was a cool area that was shaded from the hot summer sun with the branches from the live oak trees that lined both sides of the creek. The cattle walked in the cool, clear water on a regular basis. If a cow ever came up missing, the cowboys would follow the creek and usually find her strolling happily along through the water eating the green grass on its banks.

The calves in the west pasture were all heifers. They had grown considerably since last summer and would soon be ready to have their first calves. After they had their first calves, they'd no longer be called heifers. They would be cows.

Jasper got to work and guided the calves into a corral. There were fence panels which made a long tunnel that led out of the corral that were wide enough for only one calf at a time to walk through. The cowboys guided the calves through the tunnel. Sometimes the calves balked, and one of the cowboys had to give them a good swat on the behind to get them to move forward. Justin, Dallas, and Hank were given the job of helping to move the calves through. They watched the calves as they came through the chute and tried to remember them from last summer. All the calves had tags in their ears and were identified by a number. Since the calves would be sold one day soon, they tried not to think of them as pets. They seldom gave them names. They simply referred to them by their tag number.

As the calves made their way down the chute, each one received the shots it needed to stay healthy. Sometimes they got more than one shot, but they always got a good looking-over by the cowboys. They wanted the heifers to be healthy and strong before they had their first calves. The first calf by a heifer was always the hardest to deliver. She would need to be strong before she met the bull and had her first calf.

With their work done, the cowboys returned to the bunkhouse for some cool-down time in front of the air conditioner and a good hearty supper. Ms. Adaline had plenty of food for them to devour. Ace stayed at the house that afternoon to help her get things ready for supper and haul it down to the bunkhouse. The cowboys were anxious to get a plateful of Ms. Adaline's mouth-watering food along with a big quart jar of ice-cold sweet tea. After a hard day on the ranch in the hot Texas sun, they were ready for food and relaxation around the bunkhouse before calling it a day and hitting the hay.

CHAPTER 5

Mending Fences on the Double A Ranch

MORNING SEEMS TO COME EARLY on a ranch especially during the summer. The ranch hands at the Double A got up early to try to get as much work done as they could before the summer heat set in. Slim, the bunkhouse cook was the first one up every morning. He put the coffee on and started frying up the bacon and sausage for the rest of the cowboys. They didn't need an alarm clock. They woke up every morning to the good smells of breakfast.

The boys on the other hand needed more than just an alarm clock. Ole Ace took on that role. He stomped into the Cowboy Room where the boys slept. The Cowboy Room was decorated with western décor especially for the grandkids.

"Rise and shine!" he hollered at the boys. "I need some cowboys to help me out on the ranch this morning. Anybody in here want to go with me?"

Justin, Dallas, and Hank sat up in bed with wild hair and squinting eyes. It was still dark outside, but they were ready to put on their boots and jeans and ride with the cowboys.

Ms. Adaline had prepared a big breakfast for everyone. No bowls of cold cereal were ever served for breakfast on the Double A. The boys arrived at the breakfast table fully dressed except for their hats.

After breakfast, they said good-bye to Ms. Adaline, grabbed their cowboy hats, and jumped in the back of Ace's pickup. The sun was just beginning to peek over the eastern horizon of the Double A. The morning air was cool and fresh, and the birds were chattering away as they flew nervously from tree to tree. Many of the birds had nests with baby birds in them that needed to be fed, so the early birds were out looking for the worms.

Ace pulled up in front of the bunkhouse, and the boys jumped out of the back. Jasper had spotted them coming down the road and had run out to greet them with his tail wagging and his tongue hanging out. The boys bent down, gave him a couple of pats, and rubbed his silky coat. It looked like Jasper was ready to get to work.

The cowboys gathered around on the front porch of the bunkhouse. Rowdy gave the orders for the morning. Since the cattle had been moved to fresh pastures and the calves had been worked the day before, today was going to be a day of checking the fenceline and mending it wherever it was needed.

Barbed wire was stretched between the fence posts. It was used to keep the cattle on the ranch as well as mark the boundary lines of the pastures. It was strong and durable, but from time to time it needed to be repaired. Sometimes cattle smelled some grass on the other side of the barbed wire and stuck their heads through the wire to get a big mouthful. When they did, they often pulled on the wire and caused it to sag or break between the posts. The cowboys preferred to mend it before the cattle decided to jump it and visit the cattle in the neighboring pastures.

Rowdy greeted the boys, "Well, did you boys get a good night's sleep? I sure hope so 'cause we've got a lot of work to git done this mornin'."

"Yes, sir, Rowdy," said Hank. "We always sleep well on the Double A."

"I slept like a log last night," said Justin. "I suppose I won't have any trouble with sleeping after a day of working on the ranch. You know, Rowdy, we are not used to hard work like you and the other cowboys."

Rowdy smiled. "Yes, I know that. You city slickers are more used to being in a herd of cars in those pastures made of concrete and asphalt than you are to these pastures of green grass and cool creeks. But, that's all right, 'cause I git to be the one to show you around and instruct you on all the workings of a ranch. It's like I'm your teacher in this here summer school, and I'm teaching you a cowboy's way of life."

Hank, the youngest cowboy on the Double A Ranch that day, was still playing with Jasper. Hank had found an old ham bone that Jasper had been chewing on and was teasing him with it. Jasper was wiggling around while his tail was fanning the wind, just waiting for Hank to toss the bone to him. There wasn't a bit of meat left on the bone, but Jasper still liked to chew on it. Hank finally tossed the bone, and Jasper took off running for it. Instead of bringing it back to Hank, he grabbed it and ran straight for the shade of a mesquite tree. He promptly flopped down and began chewing on it.

Hank joined his big brothers. It was time to get started on their morning work. The boys got in the back of Ace's pickup and rode across the ranch. Dirt trails had been formed in the pastures over the years where the trucks and horses had worn down the grass. From time to time, the cowboys had to fill in some chug holes with rocks and dirt, but they were never smooth like the city streets. The boys thought it was a lot of fun on the bumpy roads anyway. Ace had to drive slowly and occasionally drive around a chug hole or sharp rock. At last, they made it out to a fence that needed mending.

Rowdy and a group of ranch hands on horses had already located a spot on the fence that needed mending. Rowdy had a big roll of barbed wire and a big tool box in the back of his pickup.

Rowdy called the boys over to give him a hand, "Justin, hand me one of those wire cutters from the tool box. Dallas, I need you to give me the crimpers. Hank, I want you to take these other wire cutters down to Patch."

Patch was one of the ranch hands. His beard was reddish-brown and had large spots of silver and white in it. It looked like someone had painted his beard with patches of white here and there. It looked that way ever since he was just a young man in his twenties. It was about that time Patch decided that shaving every morning was more trouble than it was worth especially since the cows on the ranch didn't seem to care if he were clean shaven or not.

Hank jumped out of the back of the pickup, took the wire cutters out of Rowdy's hand and hustled down the fenceline to give them to Patch. Hank was a little bit afraid of Patch because he only had about half of his teeth. When he smiled through that patchy beard, he showed big gaps of nothing where his teeth had once been. Hank wasn't quite sure about Patch, but it was always a good reminder to Hank to brush his teeth after breakfast and before he went to bed at night.

"Why, thank you, little buddy," said Patch. "You're as fine as the hair on a frog's back."

"You're welcome, Patch," said Hank. "Do you need me to do anything else for you?"

"No, not just yet, but why don't you find yourself a good place to sit and keep me company while I work on this fence." Patch pulled out his bandana and wiped the sweat off his forehead.

"Patch," said Hank. "Why do they call that wire 'barbed' wire?"

Patch pointed to a small piece of wire that was twisted around the double strands of wire that was stretched tightly between the fence posts. "That, young man, is a barb. It is supposed to keep the cattle away from the fence. That sharp point on the end of the barb sticks the cow, and she backs off of it. But sometimes those cows still manage to stick their heads across into the neighbor's pasture to get a bite of grass. Sometimes when that happens, the wire breaks or gets stretched. That's when we come in and do our mending."

Hank was listening to Patch while keeping an eye on Rowdy. Rowdy had Justin and Dallas running back and forth to the pick-up for tools. Jasper was running back and forth with them. Hank wished Jasper would come down to where he was with Patch.

All of a sudden Patch yelled, "Dadgumit!" Hank looked over just in time to see Patch with his finger in his mouth. "That barbed wire just bit me! Looky here at what it did to me." He showed Hank where one of the barbs on the fence had poked through his leather glove and stuck him. Patch may have been a tough ole cowboy, but he sure could let out a loud yelp whenever he got hurt. "Hank, I need you to run lickety-split and git me that first aid kit out of the pickup."

Hank took off running for the first aid kit. Ace kept one in his pickup because it seemed somebody was always getting hurt. Hank grabbed the kit and ran back to Patch.

"Okay, kid," said Patch, "you open up that kit and find some of that rubbing alcohol." Hank did just as he was told and found a small bottle of rubbing alcohol. He took off the lid and handed the bottle to Patch. He poured some of the alcohol on the cut. "You're doing good, kid," said Patch. "Now find me a Band-Aid, and I don't want one with Scooby Doo on it." Hank found a plain Band-Aid and opened it up for Patch. When Patch was bandaged up, he looked up at Hank and said, "Good job, kid. I think you should grow up to be a doctor." Hank smiled at Patch. "Now, close up that kit and git it back to the pickup."

Hank walked back over to the pickup and put the first aid kit away. Jasper ran up behind him with his tail wagging. Hank took a few minutes to play with Jasper. Patch was back at work on the fence, so Hank sat down in the shade of the pickup. Jasper stretched out beside him.

Dallas and Justin came over to sit down by Hank and Jasper. "Did Patch scare you much, Hank?" asked Dallas.

"No, not much," said Hank. "He sure looks funny when he smiles, but I like him. I think he likes for me to help him." Dallas and Justin smiled at each other. Last summer, Hank wouldn't even get close to Patch, but it looked like Hank was going to do just fine around him this year.

Justin jumped up from where he was sitting and looked out across the pasture. "Come on, guys, let's run over there by that big oak tree and see if we can find some arrowheads like we did last summer. I'll tell Ace what we want to do. I don't think he'll mind."

Justin ran up to Ace and told him what they wanted to do. Ace said, "That's fine. Just stay out of trouble."

The boys and Jasper took off running toward the tall oak tree. Years ago, their father had built a tree house up in the branches, and there were still a few boards that remained high in the tree. It wasn't much of a tree house anymore, but it was a reminder to them that their daddy had once played there and climbed up into it.

The cows enjoyed napping under the tree during the summer. It was a great spot to rest on a hot summer day, and since they were there often, you had to watch out where you stepped. One thing you have to learn about animals is that when they have to "go," they "go" right where they are. Cow paddies were all over the ranch land. Some were dry because they had been there for a while. They weren't any bother because they were just like a clump of dirt. Those fresh ones, however, were wet and sticky. Those were the ones to avoid.

"Right along here is where I found arrowheads last year," said Dallas. He was walking around and looking at the dirt hoping to spot another one.

"Is this an arrowhead?" asked Hank. He found a rock with a sharp edge. He held it up for Dallas to see.

"No, that's just an old rock. If we don't find one out here, I'll show you one when we get back to the Main House," said Dallas.

Justin walked away from the tree and closer to a nearby creek. He sat down on a large white rock and began digging in the dirt with a stick he picked up off the ground. Dallas and Hank joined him.

"Do you think Indians really lived here at one time?" asked Hank.

"Of course, they did," said Justin. "Comanche Indians lived in this part of Texas. See that big hill over there? That's called Comanche Peak. That used to be a lookout point for the Comanches. They could get up there and look for miles and miles in all directions, or they could send out signals with smoke or mirrors. Ace told me one time there were several kinds of Indians, or I should say Native Americans, who lived around here before the White Man moved in. In fact, the town of Lipan is named after a tribe of Apache."

"Do you think there are Comanches still living up there?" asked Dallas.

"No, not now, silly," said Justin. "If they did, they would be living in regular houses, working at regular jobs, and you might not even know they were Comanche."

"That's too bad," said Hank. "I bet they would have a lot of arrowheads. Justin, what *is* an arrowhead anyway?"

Dallas jumped in to answer his little brother. "An arrowhead is a piece of rock that is shaped into a point and then placed on the end of a straight stick for a weapon such as an arrow or spear. They were used for hunting and protection. They used a hard rock like flint for the arrowheads. Ace has some at the house that we can look at sometime."

The boys heard a loud whistle. They looked over their shoulders and saw Ace waving them over to the pickup. They jumped up and raced over to him.

"Come on, boys, it's time to move on to the next job," said Ace. The boys jumped into the back of the pickup along with Jasper.

Ace yelled out of his rolled down window, "Head 'em up! Move 'em out! Hang on, cowboys! This here mule is pickin' up speed."

CHAPTER 6

DAVID AND ELIZABETH CROCKETT

AFTER A LONG DAY on the ranch, Ace, the ranch hands, and the boys returned to the house to clean up and eat supper. Ms. Adaline worked most of the day around the house and later on prepared a fine supper for Ace and the boys. Ms. Adaline also made a sauerkraut cake for dessert, but she told the boys it was a chocolate cake until after they had eaten a big slice of it. They might not have eaten it if they had known there was sauerkraut in it. It was made from a recipe her mother had given to her, and everyone loved it as long as they didn't know what was in it.

After supper, the boys wandered outside. The sun was beginning to set, but the heat of the day still hung heavily in the air. The ranch at night was very different than it was during the day. All the critters that were out during the day settled in for the night, and all the other critters that came out at night were beginning to stir.

The sky was clear, and the stars were beginning to shine through the night sky like tiny twinkling diamonds. A bright full moon was the final touch to a stunning evening that formed a memory in the minds of the boys. They were always amazed at how many more stars they could see at night on the ranch than in the city.

"Let's go see what's going on at the bunkhouse," said Dallas. The boys began walking in the direction of the bunkhouse when they spotted Rowdy, Patch, and a couple of other ranch hands sitting around a campfire. They decided to join them to see what they were doing.

"Howdy, boys!" said Rowdy. "Come join us 'round this campfire. Watch out for the flyin' sparks though. They'll give ya a mighty painful kiss if you're not careful, and you boys are too young for kissin'!" Jasper got up from beside Rowdy and ran over to the boys with his tail wagging.

"Are you trying to be funny, Rowdy?" asked Justin with a shy smile on his face. "We saw your campfire and decided we'd come over and visit with you, if that's okay." The boys found a place to sit, and Jasper went back over to his spot by Rowdy.

"Why, of course it is," said Rowdy. He reached into his shirt pocket and pulled out his harmonica. He played a tune the boys recognized as "Home on the Range." Everyone else kept their eyes on the fire as it popped and cracked while Rowdy played. The boys watched him carefully as he made music from that little instrument cupped in his large, work-worn hands.

When Rowdy finished playing, Patch asked, "Did you boys have a good time today?"

"Yes, sir," said Hank. "We like working on the ranch. We looked for some arrowheads today, but we didn't find any."

"You didn't? We'll probably find some while you're visitin' here this summer," said Patch. "There are all kinds of arrowheads around the ranch. They are reminders of the days when the Caddo, Comanche, and Lipan Apache lived on this land. In fact, there are reminders all around us about the early days in Texas."

Patch looked up from the fire and said, "Do you boys know who David Crockett was?"

"Yes, sir!" said all the boys at the same time.

"Well, let me tell you some things you probably don't know about ole Crockett," said Patch. He sat up a little straighter and leaned toward the fire so he could see the boys better. The campfire made Patch look even scarier than he did in the daylight. Hank scooted closer to Justin. The campfire made a loud pop and settled back to a nice warm glow.

Patch scratched his chin through his beard and said, "David Crockett is a real Texas hero. He was just one of the many brave men who fought and died at the battle of the Alamo on March 6, 1836. Have you boys seen the Alamo? Do you know what I'm talkin' about?"

"Yes, sir," said Justin. "We've been to San Antonio to see the Alamo."

"Yeah," said Dallas. "Last summer we went to Sea World. Before we came home, we stopped by to see it."

"Well," said Patch, "that's good 'cause every Texan should see the Alamo. They should also see the mission at Goliad and the San

Jacinto Monument. There were battles in those places where common everyday folks stood up to fight against General Santa Anna and his Mexican soldiers.

"Well, David Crockett was born in Greene County, Tennessee in 1786. His mama named him David, not Davy. Nobody called him Davy until he became a legend. He probably wouldn't have liked anybody calling him 'Davy' to his face. He was an independent, self-reliant, opinionated, stubborn, cantankerous, unsophisticated, but honest backwoodsman. He had eight brothers and sisters, and his family was dirt-poor. When he was only twelve years old, his daddy hired him out as a servant. He spent several months working for a cattle drover herding cattle into Virginia. He traveled back and forth with the herds. When he got back home, he gave his father what he had earned, a full six dollars.

"Ole David married a pretty little lady named Polly. Unfortunately, she died soon after the birth of their third child. A few months later he married Elizabeth Patton, a widow-lady who had three children of her own. He tried to start up his own business a time or two, but he didn't have any success with that.

"One thing he sure could do well, though, was tell a good story. One of my favorite stories David Crockett told was a tall tale," said Patch. "I'll see if I can tell you the story the way he would have told it."

Patch stood up so he could tell the story and use his hands to demonstrate the actions of the characters. Then, he began speaking as if he were David Crockett:

One day I was huntin' in the woods and spied a big fat raccoon sittin' way up in the top of a tree. I slowly raised my rifle up to take aim, but before I could fire that rifle, that ole raccoon held up a paw as if he wanted me to stop. Then that 'coon put his other paw up to his mouth and hollered down from the tree, "Is your name Crockett?"

I nodded my head and said, "Yep, it sure is."

That 'coon hollered back to me, "Hold on there, Mr. Crockett! I've heard about you. I'll save you the gunpowder. I'm a comin' down right this minute. With you behind that rifle, I'm as good as dead anyway."

When the raccoon got to the ground, I patted that little feller on the head and said, "I sure do admire you for your wisdom and good manners, Mr. 'Coon. I think I'm just gonna let you go free."

That raccoon looked up at me and said, "If you don't mind, Mr. Crockett, I believe I'll leave right now just in case you change yore mind." And, you know what? That 'coon took off in a dash across the woods and was never, ever seen again. It was said that he told all them other raccoons he had escaped the deadly aim of the King of the Wild Frontier. I reckon that ole 'coon became the King of the Raccoons himself among all his forest fellers.

"Is that true?" asked Hank.

"Well, now what do you think, cowboy?" asked Patch.

"I don't think it is," said Hank.

"Well, cowboy, I agree with you. That's what you call one of them tall tales, and I bet ole David had a good time telling that story," laughed Patch.

"Now, let's get on with David," said Patch. "David Crockett enlisted in the Tennessee Militia during the Creek Indian War. David was such a good hunter he spent most of his time hunting food for the hungry troops. He liked using his fine hunting skills to provide food rather than fighting against the Indians, because he was really a friend to the Indians. He didn't think it was right to force them off their lands so the settlers could move in and build farms.

"Did you know David Crockett was also a politician?" asked Patch. "He became a politician in Tennessee and in Washington, D. C. He finally came to his senses after he lost his last election, and he decided to head to Texas. That was in January of 1836.

"Texas was a new frontier. Why, it wasn't even a part of the United States yet. Texas was still a part of Mexico and was a wild country with Indians and all sorts of uncivilized folks, so it took a brave person or a foolish person to enter into this frontier. David Crockett was just the kind of man that Texas needed. He was looking for an adventure, and he was brave."

"Did he really wear a coonskin cap, Patch?" asked Hank.

"Well, I guess he could have, but I doubt it," said Patch. "Over the years David Crockett became a legend thanks to a television show and some kiddy tune about him. They had him wearing a coonskin cap, but it is my understanding that he didn't wear one. At the end of the day, it don't really matter. He was brave enough to stand up to General Santa Anna and his soldiers, so it really don't matter what he had on his head."

Photo by Grace Mercado-Marx was used with permission.

The chapel of the Mission San Antonio de Valero became known as "The Alamo." The word Alamo means "Cottonwood."

Patch combed his beard with his fingers and continued, "Now you know that David was killed at the Alamo. He and all the other Texians that were killed on March 6, 1836, were buried right there at the Alamo. Why, there were men such as William B. Travis, Jim Bowie, and more. Yep, that is sacred soil around the Alamo. Santa Anna and his soldiers killed every one of those Texians except just a handful of people. Susanna Dickinson and her baby girl and about ten others survived all that fightin'. Those that survived were told to go out and tell everyone they met up with just how mean Santa Anna was. Santa Anna wanted those Texians to be afraid of him whenever they saw him comin' down the road."

"Patch, you said 'Texians,'" said Justin. "What is a Texian?"

Patch explained, "Texians were those Americans who were living in Texas. Remember now, at that time Texas still belonged to Mexico. This fightin' by the Texians was to take control of Texas. Once the battle was over at San Jacinto, ole Sam Houston and his soldiers and the other Texians with them turned Texas into the Republic of Texas. But that's another story for another campfire."

"Did David Crockett ever come up here to Hood County?" asked Dallas.

"Nope," said Patch. "He never had the pleasure of gettin' up here to Hood County, but his wife did."

"She did?" asked Hank.

"She did!" said Patch. "In fact, she lived not far from here. Her name was Elizabeth."

"But why would she come to Texas after David died?" asked Justin.

"Great question, cowboy," said Patch. "After Texas got its independence from Mexico, it thanked all the men who fought by giving them or their families some land. Yep, Ms. Crockett got a whole bunch of land right here in Indian Territory. In 1852, Ms. Crockett came to Texas with some of her grown children and grandchildren. Let's see now, there was Rebecca and her husband, Reverend James Halford; and Robert Crockett and his wife Matlida; and George Patton, his wife, and children. You see, George was born when she was married to her first husband, Mr. Patton. It was after Mr. Patton died that she married ole Crockett. She and David had some children of their own.

"After Mrs. Crockett and her family came to Texas to claim their land, they lived near Waxahachie in Ellis County for a couple of years. Then they loaded up and moved up here to Hood County. This became their home, and their children and grandchildren grew up and became responsible citizens here in Hood County. Rev. Halford, the husband of Rebecca Crockett, was the second pastor at Acton Baptist Church, a church not too far from here. That's when the church was just a small building and several church groups took turns using it.

"Can you boys imagine how hard it must have been for Ms. Crockett to sell her farm in Tennessee, load up all her belongings, head across the country from Tennessee, and walk or ride in a bumpy, dusty, old wagon? They had to battle the sun, wind, and rain all the way to Texas. She didn't know exactly where she was going or what she was gonna find when she got here, but she did it anyway. Now that was one brave lady."

"Did she live close to this ranch?" asked Dallas.

"Yep, she sure did," said Patch. "In fact, one day I'll show you where she lived. Her son, Robert, first built a log cabin for all of them to live in. I think it only had two rooms in it, but it gave them shelter until he could build his mom a place of her own."

"That's cool," said Justin. "She's not still alive, is she?"

Photo by Nancy Sifford Alana

Elizabeth Crockett Statue, Acton Cemetery, Acton, TX

"No, she died in 1860. She went for a walk one fine morning in January, collapsed, and died. She's buried out there in the Acton Cemetery. There's a big statue out there that shows her with one hand shading her eyes as she looks for David to come home to her." Patch put his left hand over his eyes to show them how she looks on the statue. "I guess she finally found him up in heaven."

Patch shifted his legs. The boys could tell he had been sitting too long, and his legs were getting stiff. He stood up, shook each leg to get the blood circulating again, and said, "Maybe one day we can take you boys out there so you can pay your respects to Ms. Crockett. Officially, the Acton Cemetery is the smallest state park in Texas."

"That's a great story, Patch," said Hank. "Do you know anyone who knew her?"

"No, Hank, I don't, but I do know one of her great-great grandsons," said Patch.

"No way!" said Dallas. "Really?"

"Why, sure I do!" said Patch. "He lives out there in Acton with his sweet wife. His name is Ken Hendricks, and his wife is Ms. Jessie. Mr. Hendricks even dresses up like David Crockett from time to time for special events like parades and such. He and Ms. Jessie are the nicest people you could ever hope to know."

Photo by Nancy Sifford Alana

Kenneth Hendricks, great-great grandson of David and Elizabeth Crockett, and his wife, Jessie

"Well, boys," said Rowdy, "Patch has told you a mighty good story, but it's time for these old cowboys to hit the hay. We've got work to do in the morning. Now, you boys high-tail it over to Ace's before he comes lookin' for you."

"Yes, sir," the boys said. They stood up and turned toward the Main House. They saw Ace and Ms. Adaline sitting out front in their porch swing watching the stars.

"Happy trails, cowboys, and thanks for the company," said Patch.

The boys started walking toward the Main House. They looked back over their shoulders and shouted, "Happy trails!"

CHAPTER 7
A GIRL ON THE RANCH

ON THE THIRD DAY at the Double A Ranch, the boys woke up to a big rooster in their bedroom. Actually, it was Ace. He came into the bedroom strutting like a rooster with his arms bent at the elbows and hands tucked into his arm pits to look like wings. He strutted close to the bed and shouted, "Cock-a-doodle-do, cock-a- doodle-do! The sun is up, and all cowboys should be, too."

Dallas jumped out of bed first, ran toward Ace, and tried to tackle him. It didn't work, but they had a good laugh over it. Justin and Hank sat up in bed and laughed. Ace was such a funny grandfather!

After a good breakfast, Ms. Adaline sent the cowboys off to work with a container of homemade chocolate chip cookies. Later on in the morning, the boys could eat them as a snack.

The boys jumped in the back of Ace's pickup for the short ride over to the bunkhouse. While the boys were waiting for Ace to rev up the engine and take off, they noticed a red SUV coming down the drive toward the Main House.

"Ace, somebody's coming down the drive," said Justin. "Are you expecting company?"

"Naw, but that might be my neighbors from down the road," said Ace. "Let me see what they want."

Ace opened the door of the pickup and got out. He greeted his neighbor, listened to him for a minute, and said, "Dallas, would you please go get Ms. Adaline?"

Dallas jumped out of the back of the pickup and ran into the house. When he came out, Ms. Adaline was with him. She walked over to Ace, and Dallas climbed back into the pickup bed. She talked with her neighbor, nodded her head, and then the passenger door to the SUV opened. A girl about ten years old got out of the vehicle. Ms. Adaline walked over to her, and then they approached the pickup where the boys were waiting and wondering what was going on.

"Boys," said Ms. Adaline. "This is Jennie. She lives down the road, and she's going to be spending the day with us."

The boys looked at each other then back at Jennie. A girl? On the Double A?

"Now, you boys be nice to Jennie. Her mama is on her way to the hospital to have a baby."

"Okay," they said, although Ms. Adaline could tell the boys weren't too excited about having a girl tag along with them.

"Jennie, these are my grandsons. This is Justin, Dallas, and Hank. They are visiting from the city for a few days."

Jennie definitely had a cowgirl's sense of fashion. She wore Wrangler jeans that were tucked into her red ropers, a long-sleeved white shirt that was crisply starched and tucked in at the waist, and a black felt cowboy hat. She sported a red bandana around her neck. Her hair was long and wavy and tied back into a pony tail. She felt quite comfortable climbing into the back of the pickup. It looked as if she had done it many times before.

She looked the boys over, and said, "Well, you look like you've never seen a cowgirl! Don't worry about me. I know my way around, and I won't get in your way. In fact, whatever you think you can do on this ranch, I can probably do better."

Once again, the boys looked at each other and raised their eyebrows as a way of saying, "This should be interesting."

Ace got back in the pickup and shouted, "Hold on, cowboys! This here mule is pickin' up speed."

At the bunkhouse, Rowdy gave out the working orders for the day. Half of the cowboys were told to finish working on the fenceline, and the other cowboys were told it was time to work at the horse barn. Horses must be groomed on a regular basis. They need to be curried and brushed. Their hooves need to be cleaned and checked out regularly.

"You kids come with me to the horse barn," said Rowdy. Jennie and the boys smiled. That is exactly what they were hoping he would say.

Ace returned to the Main House to help Ms. Adaline. He had been slowly turning over the running of the ranch to Rowdy for the past four years. That was when he had been very ill, and he realized he couldn't do what he used to around the ranch. He was still the boss, but he had Rowdy make the day-to-day decisions and do the work that required heavy lifting. Unfortunately that was almost all of the work on the ranch. Thank goodness he had some good ranch hands to help him out.

Jennie was happy to go to the horse barn. She had not told the boys yet that she had a horse of her own. Her horse was used for barrel racing. She was an excellent rider, but that was nothing to brag about, so she kept that information to herself.

Rowdy had an old pickup that he drove when he worked on the ranch. It was an old Chevrolet pickup that was dented, dirty, and dinged. It needed a paint job, but Rowdy didn't want to spend any money on it unless it was necessary. Justin grabbed the container of cookies, and the kids jumped into the back of the pickup for the ride over to the horse barn.

Once they were there, Rowdy told the kids, "Y'all stay close to me. We're going to bring the horses out of the barn to groom them. Jennie, you know how this works. Come on, and I'll git a horse for you. Boys, you stay here."

Rowdy led a horse out of the barn for Jennie to work on. All the supplies she needed were in a large bucket. She got busy with the curry brush using small round strokes to loosen the dirt and sweat from the horse. Jennie didn't get in a hurry because the horse was not familiar with her. She talked to him and kept her hand on him, so he always knew where she was standing. She didn't want the horse to get spooked or try to kick her, so she worked slowly and gave the horse plenty of room when she walked behind him. The kick of a horse could break a bone or cause some real damage to even the strongest cowboy.

Rowdy walked back into the barn for another horse. He led out a beautiful black horse named Beau. He looked strong and healthy.

He walked with a prance and tossed his head from side to side as Rowdy led him to a place along the corral where he would be hitched. Rowdy had to hold on to the reins tightly as they walked. The boys were always amazed at the strength and power of a well-cared for horse.

After Beau was securely tied to a rail on the corral, Rowdy went after a bucket of supplies. He told the boys to do what Jennie was doing while he went to check on the other hands. The boys stood there and looked at each other for a few seconds before Justin picked up the bucket and took out the curry brush. He began brushing Beau just like Jennie brushed her horse by starting at the horse's head and moving back to the tail.

"Jennie, I didn't know you knew how to groom a horse," said Dallas.

"When you live on a ranch with horses, you have to know how," said Jennie. "I have to take care of my horse every day."

"You have a horse?" asked Hank.

Jennie smiled and said, "Yeah, her name is Gypsy. I ride her every day."

"You're lucky," said Hank. "I wish I had a horse. I'd name him Domingo."

"Domingo is a great name for a horse, Hank," said Jennie. "I hope you have a horse of your own one of these days. Maybe you can come over to my house soon. I'll show Gypsy to you and then show you how to do barrel racing."

"What's barrel racing?" asked Justin.

"It's a race to see who can run a clover-leaf pattern around three barrels the fastest," said Jennie.

About that time, Rowdy came by to check on the boys. He cleaned the hooves of both the horses. Then, he led the horses to a trough for a drink of cool water.

"Okay, kids, let's muck the stalls," said Rowdy. "Everybody grab either a shovel or a pitchfork except Hank. Hank, I need you to get me a wheelbarrow."

Mucking the stalls meant they would scoop up the straw and manure, and replace it with clean straw. It wasn't a pleasant job, but it had to be done daily in order to keep the stalls clean enough for the horses to sleep in.

Hank found a wheelbarrow and managed to roll it down to the stall where everyone else was working. "Yuck," said Hank. "It stinks in here."

"You'll get used to the smell," said Jennie. She was ready to dump a loaded down pitchfork into the wheelbarrow. Hank wrinkled up his nose when he saw it.

After the stall was cleaned, Rowdy brought in some clean straw and scattered it around on the floor. Then they moved on to the next one. Whenever the wheelbarrow was full, Rowdy would tell Hank to take it out behind the barn and dump it. After several stalls, the boys were ready for a break. It seemed like the perfect time to bring out Ms. Adaline's cookies.

"I'll go get the cookies," said Justin.

"Go wash your hands first," yelled Rowdy. "There's a place to wash up outside the barn. Come on, kids. If we're going to eat some of Ms. Adaline's cookies, we all need to wash up."

Justin got the cookies out of the pickup. He was thankful he remembered to get them out of Ace's pickup before they left the bunkhouse. He ran back to where the others were washing up.

"Well, boys, what do you think of these horses?" asked Rowdy.

"They are a lot of work!" said Dallas. "I'd like to have a horse someday."

"Horses *are* a lot of work," said Jennie. "Not only do you have to feed and groom them every day, but you also have to exercise them. I love it, and I look forward to spending time with Gypsy. She's a part of my family."

After eating a couple of Ms. Adaline's chocolate chip cookies, Rowdy stood up and told the kids to go with him in the pickup. They jumped in the back, and Rowdy drove away from the horse barn toward another old barn. The old barn was not in good condition. It had boards missing here and there, and it seemed to lean a little bit, but it was good enough to store things in. Rowdy opened the double doors of the barn so the kids could look in. There were stacks and stacks of junk everywhere.

"Wow! This is cool!" said Justin. "Where did all of this stuff come from?"

"Most of it belongs to Ace and Ms. Adaline. Whenever something breaks or gets replaced with something new, we haul it out here for them. We've been doin' this for years, so there's no tellin' what we'll find in all this mess. Ace always says, 'It's better to have it and not need it, than to need it and not have it,'" said Rowdy.

"Are you looking for something in particular in here?" asked Jennie.

"There's an old foot locker in here somewhere that I'd like to find," said Rowdy. "It belonged to my granddaddy. When I first moved onto the Double A many years ago, I put it in here. Over the years, a lot of other stuff has been stored in here. Since we had a few minutes before we head back to the bunkhouse for lunch, I thought I'd stop in and look around."

"What's a foot locker?" asked Hank.

"It's a chest that has three locks on it that you store things in. The middle lock must be opened with a key. I think you'll know it when you see it," said Rowdy. "Let's scatter out and see if we can find it."

The kids did just as Rowdy suggested and started walking around through all the junk. Most of it was stored in boxes, but a lot of it was just lying around collecting dust. There were old clothes, furniture, glass jars, old tires, and a lot of stuff they didn't recognize. After about fifteen minutes, Rowdy said, "Well, it's time for lunch. Let's head back up to the bunkhouse."

After lunch, Rowdy told the kids they could take the afternoon off. It was getting hot, and Rowdy decided it might be too much for them to handle. With time on their hands, the kids decided to go exploring.

"Let's go back to the old barn and see what we can find," said Justin.

"Yeah, I like that idea," said Jennie. "I bet there are some really cool things in there."

As they walked across the pasture to the barn, Justin asked, "How do you catch a squirrel?"

"Why do you want to catch a squirrel?" asked Dallas.

"It's a joke, silly," said Justin. "How do you catch a squirrel?"

"I don't know. How?"

"Climb a tree and act like a nut!" said Justin. Everyone laughed, but Justin laughed the hardest of all. He always laughed at his own jokes even if no one else did.

Without missing a beat, Justin asked another question, "What do you get if you cross a cow with a grass cutter?"

"I don't know," said Jennie. "What?"

"A lawn mooer!"

"I've got one," said Hank. "What do you call a box of ducklings?"

"I give up," said Dallas. "What?"

"A box of quackers!" laughed Hank.

"You guys are funny! Not!" said Jennie. "It's a good thing we're at the barn. I don't think I could take any more of your silly jokes."

Justin opened the doors to the barn and left them wide open so they could have enough light to see what they were looking at inside the dark barn. They decided to spread out in all directions and try to find one really unique item to take to the campfire that night. They would ask Rowdy and Patch to judge who had the best item of all.

It was kind of creepy in the barn. From time to time, they would hear something running around in a pile of junk. They figured it was a mouse or a rat, but it might have been a raccoon or a possum. Hank was trying to be brave, but he was leery of what he might find hiding underneath something when he picked it up. The barn creaked when the wind blew, and made things worse as far as Hank was concerned.

Dallas spotted a box of old toys. He sorted through them and found old trucks, model horses, army men, Star Wars figures, and Matchbox cars. He sat the box on the dirt floor of the barn and squatted down beside it. He took everything out of the box to see if there was something he could take to the campfire that night. He really liked the Star Wars figures and a model of a covered wagon with the letters G-T-T on it. He needed to make a decision soon.

Justin found an old chest of drawers. He pulled out one drawer, and it was empty. The second drawer had old magazines and newspapers. The magazine on top was a *Life* magazine from 1972. The third drawer had some old clothes in it, but the fourth drawer was the jackpot. There were boxes and boxes of old baseball and Pokémon cards. Justin's dad had told him about all the cards he'd collected as a kid, but he had no idea what had happened to them. Now, Justin could tell him where they were. He sat down on the floor and looked at some of the cards.

Jennie opened several boxes and found nothing of interest to her. She was about to give up and move to another part of the barn when she found a slender black case. She blew the dust off the top of it and opened it up. Inside the case was an old fiddle and bow. Now, that was really cool! Her grandfather had given her a few lessons on his fiddle. She picked it up and plucked the strings. It made a terrible sound!

"What was that?" asked Hank. His eyes were as big as saucers, and he looked up into the rafters and around the barn to see if he could tell where the noise was coming from. Surely the barn wasn't haunted.

"Look what I found!" said Jennie. "It's an old fiddle!"

"I wish I could find something neat. I haven't found anything yet," Hank said with a sigh.

"You're bound to find something, Hank. Just keep looking," encouraged Jennie. She found a place to sit down on a box and tried to tune the strings. She already knew what she was going to take to the campfire tonight.

Hank wandered around and finally spotted an old red Radio Flyer wagon, but there were boxes stacked in it. "Justin, will you come help me?" asked Hank.

Justin went over to see what Hank wanted. "Would you help me move these boxes?"

"Sure," said Justin. He moved the boxes out so Hank could get to the wagon.

"Thanks, Justin. This is what I'm taking to the campfire tonight!" Hank was proud of his discovery.

"Okay, everybody, let's decide on what we're going to take to show Rowdy and Patch tonight," said Justin. "Maybe we can come back tomorrow and find some other things."

They each selected one item for the campfire after supper. They walked back to the Main House with Dallas pulling Hank in the wagon. They were excited about showing off their treasures to everyone. It would be interesting to hear what Rowdy and Patch thought about them. Hopefully, Jennie would be able to stay long enough to join the boys at the campfire.

CHAPTER 8

WAGONS, EMPRESARIOS, AND THE FATHER OF TEXAS

MS. ADALINE prepared another delicious supper for the family. Jennie joined them because her mother had not had the baby yet. She was glad she would be able to stay longer at the Double A Ranch and go to the campfire with the boys. She was anxious to show Rowdy and Patch the fiddle she'd found in the old barn.

"Well, I heard you kids had fun in the old junk barn today," said Ace. "I hope you didn't find any critters in there. The last time I was in there I thought I heard a rat running around."

"We didn't find any critters," said Jennie, "but Hank said he heard something."

"I heard something, but I never did see anything. It might have been a rat," said Hank. "Ace, I found an old wagon in the barn. Can I play with it?"

"Sure, you can," said Ace. "That wagon belonged to your daddy. He used to pull that thing all over the place. One time he filled it full of rocks of all different shapes and sizes, and then he stood out by the entrance to the ranch with a sign that said, 'Rocks for Sale.' I think he sold about a dollar's worth of rocks to somebody. I can't imagine why they wanted to pay money for a rock, but they did, and your daddy was happy."

"Hey, that's a good idea. Maybe I could do that," said Hank. He was always looking for a way to earn some extra money.

"We all found something in the old barn that we wanted to show Rowdy and Patch at the campfire tonight. Is it okay with you if we go back to the campfire later?" asked Justin.

"Why, I don't care," said Ace. "Those cowboys have all sorts of stories they could tell you. They might even have some stories about those things you found today. What did you find, Dallas?"

"I found a model of a covered wagon," said Dallas. Ace nodded as if he knew what Dallas was talking about.

"I found some old baseball cards!" said Justin excitedly. "Daddy told us he used to collect them, but he didn't know where they were. He'll be glad to know I found them."

Ace looked over at Jennie who was chowing down on Ms. Adaline's delicious macaroni and cheese. "Well, Jennie, did you find anything?"

"Yes, sir, I did!" said Jennie very proudly. "I found an old fiddle. Do you know where it came from?"

"Well, now, that fiddle belonged to my granddaddy. He used to play the fiddle at barn dances in his younger days. People from all around the county would come out to his barn for some socializing. They'd git all dressed up and git there however they could. Some rode horses. Some came in wagons. Some even walked or had a vehicle of some sort to ride in. However they got there, they had a good time dancin' and visitin' with friends they hadn't seen in a while. Granddaddy said he used to play the fiddle, and there were some others who played a fiddle or guitar or bass fiddle."

"Who wants dessert?" asked Ms. Adaline as she stood up to go into the kitchen.

She heard everyone around the table say "I do!" She served up a big portion of warm pecan pie with a scoop of vanilla ice cream on top.

"Now that's what I call deeee-licious," said Ace. "Yep, there's no other word to describe it. It is simply delicious. There's only one thing better than pecan pie, and that's warm pecan pie with a big scoop of Blue Bell ice cream on top."

"That's Mrs. Meek's recipe," said Ms. Adaline. "She has always made wonderful pecan pies. I finally asked her if I could have the recipe. That's why I need you to pick up those pecans in the fall, Ace. No pecans, no pecan pies!"

"Ms. Adaline, I will never complain again about pickin' up those pecans," said Ace.

After supper, Jennie and the boys helped Ms. Adaline clear the table and clean up the kitchen. Then they went outside to see if the cowboys had made it over to the campfire. The fire was just getting started, so they gathered up their treasures and headed over to join Rowdy, Patch, and a few other cowboys who were already settling in for a relaxing time.

"Well, looky here who's comin,'" said Patch. "Howdy, cow-pokes. How 'bout joinin' us?"

The boys and Jennie found a place to sit close to Rowdy and Patch. They each had a treasure with them, and each one hoped Rowdy and Patch would like theirs the best.

Rowdy looked over at Jennie and said, "Jennie, it was good to have you on the Double A today. It's been a long time since I had the pleasure of your company. I heard your mama was on her way to the hospital. Did she have the baby yet?"

"No, sir," said Jennie. "Not yet."

"Well, she'll have that baby when the time is right," said Rowdy.

Hank ended up sitting by Patch. He reached back to pull the wagon in closer to where he was sitting. "Whatcha got there, cow-boy?" asked Patch.

"I found this wagon in the old barn today," said Hank. "Ace said it used to belong to my daddy."

"Did you go digging 'round in that old barn today?" asked Patch as he ran his hand over his beard to smooth some wild hairs.

Justin jumped in to answer Patch. "Yes, sir, we did. We brought some things to show you and Rowdy. We were wondering if y'all would look at what we brought and tell us which one is the best."

"Why, sure we will!" said Patch. "It may be hard to tell which one is the best, but I want to see what you found."

"Did you find my footlocker?" asked Rowdy.

"No, sir," said Dallas. "We didn't find your footlocker, but we'll look tomorrow." Dallas was looking for a good excuse to go through some more of that junk. He secretly hoped they didn't find Rowdy's footlocker for a few more days.

Rowdy said, "Okay, show me what you found."

They let Jennie go first since she was a girl, and because she was a guest. She reached behind her for the black case, opened it up, and pulled out the old fiddle.

"Well, Jiminy Cricket!" said Patch. "Jennie found herself a fiddle!"

"I found this old fiddle, and Ace told us at supper that it belonged to his granddaddy who played it at barn dances," said Jennie.

"Well, ain't that somethin'?" said Patch. "Here, let me take a look at that fiddle." He reached over to get it from Jennie. He plucked the strings, made a few adjustments with the pegs and said, "That should be pretty close. Now, hand me that bow, and check to see if there's any rosin in that case." Jennie looked in the case and found a small box, but she didn't know what was in it. She handed it to Patch.

Patch opened the box of rosin and ran the hair of the bow through it a few times. Then he picked up the fiddle and played a few notes. It was obvious that he knew what he was doing. He started playing a lively tune, and Rowdy reached for his harmonica and joined in. Jennie and the boys smiled as everyone around the camp site tapped their feet in time with the music.

When they finished playing, Patch said, "Well, Jennie, you found a mighty fine fiddle in that old barn." He handed it back to her, and she put it back into the case.

"I'm next," said Hank. "I found this red wagon. Ace said when my daddy was a little boy he filled it full of rocks and sold them out by the entrance gate."

"Yep," said Rowdy. "I remember when he did that. He worked all day gathering those rocks. The next morning he got up early and made a sign that said 'Rocks for Sale.' Then he sat out there in the hot sun tryin' to git people to stop and buy one of his rocks. It was as hot as the dickens that day. Finally, a little lady from down the road stopped. She picked out a couple of rocks and paid him a dollar. That made him happy, and he pulled that wagon back down to the Main House. I think he dumped those rocks in the yard, and Ms. Adaline put them in a flower bed. You found a good thing in that barn, didn't you, Hank?"

"Yes, sir," said Hank. "Dallas even pulled me in it today, and it works just fine."

"And, you got a free ride? You are one lucky fellow!" said Patch with a grin. Hank nodded.

"Okay, I'll go next," said Justin. He opened up a long slender box of Topps baseball cards. "I found an old chest of drawers in the barn, and in the bottom drawer were baseball and Pokémon cards. My dad told me about his card collection, but he didn't know where it was. Some of the cards were in boxes like this one, and some were in plastic sheets in notebooks. I don't know how many were in there, but the drawer was full."

"Yes, sir," said Rowdy. "That sounds like a mighty fine collection of cards. Let me see what you've got there." Justin handed the box of cards to Rowdy. "Let me pull out a few of these and see what I find." He sorted through the cards and pulled out a few of them while everyone else watched. "Okay, here ya go. Here's Reggie Jackson, Wade Boggs, Sammy Sosa, and Dave Madagan. Now these guys were mighty fine at playing baseball. These cards might be worth about a dollar or so each, but most of these cards in this box are of players who never made it big. It's a good collection, though, and there's no tellin' what else is in that drawer. Your daddy will be proud of you, Justin."

The last one to show his discovery from the old barn was Dallas. The covered wagon was setting in his lap. He looked down at it, and said, "It's my turn. I found this model of a covered wagon with the letters G-T-T written on the cloth that covers the top of the wagon." He held it out so Rowdy and Patch could see it.

Rowdy reached out and took it from him, but Patch was the one who got all excited about it. "Now, this has a story I bet you'd like to hear. Yep, there's a good Texas story right here. Let me see that," said Patch as he reached out to get the covered wagon from Rowdy.

He took a minute to look it over and said, "Well, let's start with G-T-T. That stands for 'Gone to Texas.' When people across the South decided to leave their homes and come to Texas, they painted the letters G-T-T on the doors of their houses so their neighbors would know what happened to them. It looks like this here wagon is supposed to represent a wagon loaded down with people headed to Texas.

"Anybody here know what an empresario is?" asked Patch. No one around the campfire knew the answer, so Patch kept on talking. "An empresario is an agent. Now you are probably wondering what that has to do with this here covered wagon. Well, I'm fixin' to tell ya," said Patch. He shifted his legs and rubbed his beard.

"A whole bunch of the early settlers in Texas were from the southern states, and they came to Texas because of an empresario named Stephen F. Austin. Now, anybody ever hear of him?"

"Yes, sir," said Jennie. "He is also called the Father of Texas."

"Well now, you're one smart gal, Jennie," said Patch.

"Austin recruited men with families to come to Texas. If they did, they got some land. Farmers got 177 acres and ranchers got 4,428 acres. Austin signed up about three hundred families and gave them a date when they would head to Texas. That gave the men time to settle things with their families, load up their wagons, and get in line for a long trip. Austin got in the front and led them all the way to Texas.

"Now remember, Texas was still part of Mexico, so Stephen F. Austin had to have permission from Mexico to do this. It really all started with Stephen's dad. His name was Moses Austin. Moses went to Mexico City and got permission to give away some of their land to American families. Mexico wanted people to move in and settle this land. But, Moses Austin died not long after he got permission to bring in the settlers. In his will, he turned his empresario business over to his son, Stephen.

"Well, not long after they got here things started going badly for Mexico. The settlers didn't want to be a part of Mexico anymore. They wanted to be independent and decide on their own laws and such. Then all the fightin' broke out, and it just so happened that Stephen F. Austin was in New Orleans when the big battle took place in San Jacinto.

"Austin wanted to be elected President of the new Republic of Texas, but he lost the election to Sam Houston. Austin became the Secretary of State under President Houston, but just a few months later, Austin got pneumonia and died in West Columbia, Texas. He was buried down there, but in 1910, they brought his body up to the city of Austin and buried him in the Texas State Cemetery.

Photo by Nancy Sifford Alana

Stephen F. Austin Monument, Texas State Cemetery, Austin, TX

"Just as Jennie said, Stephen F. Austin was called the 'Father of Texas.' The first person to call him that was Sam Houston. He gave Austin that title because the growth in Texas was a result of the three hundred families he brought to Texas. It started a population boom that has kept on going right to this day. It wasn't until then that Texas began to grow and develop into what was to become the Republic of Texas.

"Now, let me say one more thing here. Some people spend their whole lives sittin' in the shade of a tree sipping on sweet tea watchin' other people do all the work, and other people git up and work hard and make a difference. What do you think Stephen F. Austin did?"

Dallas raised his hand. "I know. He got out from under the tree and made a difference."

"Bingo! That's the right answer, cowboy. Now, which one are y'all goin' to do? Don't answer me right now, but think about it, and one of these day I want y'all to come back and tell me," said Patch.

Jimbo, one of the ranch hands at the campfire, looked over at Patch, shook his head and said, "Patch, how come you know so much about Texas?"

He took his finger and tapped his head and said, "You think this here brain don't know anything 'cept takin' care of cows? This brain is like a fine working computer. It stores everything I ever see, hear, or read." The folks around the campfire laughed at Patch. "Naw, actually I learned all this stuff from books and school. These are stories every good Texan should know."

Rowdy stood up, kicked some dirt on the campfire, and said, "Well, you young cowpokes found some mighty good things today. Now, as far as pickin' out the best, I can't do that because they were all top-notch, but I think we should do this again. Why don't you young folks bring us something else tomorrow night? We'll pick Patch's brain and see what else he has stored in that 'fine working computer' of his."

Jennie and the boys smiled and nodded at each other. They liked that idea.

"I see Ace standing on his front porch," said Rowdy. "You young cowpokes need to git your things and git on over there. Day is done, gone the sun, time for bed, that's all I said. Happy trails, folks." Rowdy tipped his cowboy hat and the other cowboys followed suit.

It had been a good day, but as the saying goes, "All good things must come to an end." A good night's sleep would come easily to the cowboys and cowgirls on the Double A.

CHAPTER 9

FROM BARN DUST TO THE DUST BOWL

MS. ADALINE made a bed on the sofa for Jennie. Her mother delivered a healthy baby boy late that evening. Ms. Adaline told Jennie's parents she would take care of her until they came home from the hospital.

Jennie woke up early the next morning when she heard Ms. Adaline in the kitchen. She was making coffee and frying some bacon. Jennie wandered into the kitchen and sat down at the table.

"Good morning, Jennie," said Ms. Adaline.

"Good morning, Ms. Adaline. Thank you for letting me sleep over here last night. I can hardly wait to see my new little brother. Daddy told me on the phone last night that his name is Jackson Christopher Dilka."

"He's lucky to have you as a big sister. You'll be a big help to your mother," said Ms. Adaline.

Ace came into the kitchen, poured himself a cup of hot coffee, and sat down at the table with Jennie. "Good morning, ladies. That bacon sure smells good this morning. Miss Jennie, did you get any sleep last night?" asked Ace.

"Yes, sir," said Jennie. "Thank you for letting me sleep over last night. I slept very well on the sofa."

Ace had not seen Jennie in a while, and he used this opportunity to get caught up with what had been going on with her. He asked, "What grade are you in now, Jennie?"

"Fourth grade."

"Fourth grade? Well, I'll be, girl!" said Ace. "It seems like only yesterday you were starting kindergarten."

Jennie smiled at Ace as she swallowed a sip of orange juice.

Ace took a sip of his hot coffee and added another teaspoon of sugar to it. "I heard you were gettin' pretty good on that horse of yours," said Ace.

"Yes, sir," said Jennie. "I practice every day, and Gypsy and I are working really hard to get better."

Ace listened closely as Jennie told him about Gypsy. She was quick around the barrels and strong enough to pick up speed quickly. She displayed all the qualities of a champion barrel racing horse. Jennie loved telling Ace and Ms. Adaline about Gypsy and dreaming of all the possible championships in the future.

It wasn't long before the boys were up. They were dressed to go out on the ranch and work, but what they really wanted to do was go back to the junk barn. After breakfast, they walked over to the bunkhouse with Jennie. They wanted to see what the ranch hands were going to be doing, and then make a decision about asking if they could go exploring in the barn again.

Rowdy sent two of the ranch hands into town to buy some supplies. He sent four out to check on the cattle, and the other ranch hands were told to clean up the bunkhouse. Rowdy asked Jennie and the boys to help him with some chores inside the bunkhouse.

When they got inside, Rowdy directed them over to an area where there were shelves of books. He said, "Last night, we were kidding Patch about how much he knows about Texas. Let me tell you a few things about Patch that he'll never tell you himself.

"Patch grew up on a ranch just down the road from where I grew up. His daddy and granddaddy owned a big ranch in South Texas, and they were good friends with my parents. Patch learned to work cattle and ride a horse when he was just a little boy. He's been a cowboy all of his life.

"Patch is also one of the smartest guys I have ever known. Believe it or not, he went to college. After he earned his bachelor's degree, he kept right on studying and got his master's degree, but all he ever really wanted to do was work on a ranch. He could have gone to a big city and gotten a job that paid a lot more than he is making out here, but he chose to be a ranch hand.

"Patch studied history when he was in college, and it's just like he said last night. If he sees it, hears it, or reads it, he remembers it. Now, I don't know how many books are on these shelves right here, but if I had to guess I'd say between three and four hundred. Almost all of these books have to do with Texas or U. S. history or ranching. Patch has read every one of these books at least once."

Rowdy sat down on an ottoman close to the book shelves, and continued, "I also want you to know that Patch is one of the finest men I have ever known. He don't look very pretty, but Patch will never do you wrong. If you ever need anything when we are out working, if you can't locate me, you look for Patch.

"Let me tell you one more thing about Patch. While he was away at college, his daddy and granddaddy died. They were ridin' in their pickup on their way to town and had a bad accident. When Patch went back to the ranch after the accident, he just couldn't stand not havin' his family there. He loaded up some of his stuff, came over to my daddy's ranch, and moved in with us. He got somebody to take care of his daddy's ranch while he went to college, but then he sold it. After he came to live with us, he only left our ranch long enough to finish up at college, but when he did that he came back to our ranch. When I came to Hood County and got a job on the Double A, Patch came along with me. We've both been here so long that Ace and Ms. Adaline are more like family to us than our real family."

"What happened to Patch's mother?" asked Dallas.

"She died when Patch was about knee-high to a grasshopper. She got real sick and never got any better. Patch can't even remember her," said Rowdy.

"That's sad," said Justin.

"Yes, it is," said Rowdy, "but he doesn't want you feeling sorry for him. He is thankful for everything he has and for all the people in his life. He doesn't ask for anything from anybody unless he just has to. He told me last night that he enjoyed having you kids here on the Double A. He said it reminded him of his daddy and granddaddy telling him stories around the campfire when he was a kid. So, I want you to spend as much time as you can in that old barn and find some more things to bring to the campfire. Let's see how many stories Patch can come up with. Patch has a lot to teach us, so let's give him the chance."

"Yes, sir," said Hank. "We were kinda hoping you'd let us go back to the junk barn today."

"Well, I don't know about tomorrow, but as far as today goes, you should high-tail it over to that barn right now and git to looking," said Rowdy. "Now, don't forget about my footlocker. I'm still hoping to find that thing."

"We'll keep looking for it," said Jennie. "Are you guys ready? Let's get on over there while it is still kind of cool."

They took off running to the old barn. They each found an area of the barn to search. After about an hour, they decided to take a break and go outside for some fresh air. They had been stirring up the dust in the barn, and it needed to settle before they stirred up some more.

"Hank, have you found anything to take to the campfire tonight?" asked Justin.

"Not really," said Hank. "I found a box of sea shells and rocks. Dad must have really liked rocks when he was a kid."

"Sometimes rocks have fossils in them," said Jennie. "I've got some at home. There used to be dinosaurs around here. Over in Glen Rose, there are some dinosaur footprints in some rocks at Dinosaur Valley State Park. It's down on the Paluxy River. They have two life-size models of dinosaurs close to the entrance of the park."

Photo by Nancy Sifford Alana

Dinosaur Valley State Park, Glen Rose, TX

"Really?" asked Dallas. "Have you been there?"

"Sure," said Jennie. "There is also Dinosaur World. They also have life-size models of dinosaurs. Maybe we can get Ace and Ms. Adaline to take us there one day while you're here."

"Dinosaurs are cool!" said Hank. "They are really giant lizards, and I like trying to catch lizards."

"Hank, have you ever seen a horned toad?" asked Dallas. "Some people even call them horned frogs. They used to run around all over the place in Texas, but there aren't as many of them as there used to be. Maybe we'll find one while we're here."

"Did anyone else find anything interesting?" asked Jennie.

"Not really, but I did find an old tool box. I'm going to go through it some more when we go back in," said Justin.

"I only found some old dishes and kitchen stuff," said Dallas. "I hope I can find something really good for Patch to talk about."

"I'm ready to go back inside the barn," said Jennie. "Is anyone else ready?"

The others followed Jennie, and the search began once again. After a little while, Rowdy stuck his head in the barn, and said, "Come on, guys, let's go have some lunch. Slim has been cooking up some hamburgers, and they sure do smell good."

The kids stopped what they were doing and followed Rowdy back to the bunkhouse. Slim was standing at the outdoor grill cooking some hamburger patties. As the cowboys came by, he gave each one a plate with a hamburger bun and grilled hamburger patty. They took their plates into the bunkhouse to load their hamburgers with lettuce, tomatoes, pickles, and onions. A big pitcher of sweet tea was ready to be poured into the quart-sized jars loaded with ice. When everyone was served, Patch said the blessing and the cowboys began to eat.

The kids found a place at one of the tables close to Patch. He looked over at them, and said, "I hope you've found something good to bring to the campfire tonight."

"We're trying to find something good," said Jennie. "We've stirred up so much dust in that barn that it looked like the Dust Bowl in there."

"Now, how do you know about the Dust Bowl, young lady?" asked Patch.

"My great-granddaddy used to live up in the Texas Panhandle near Oklahoma. He used to tell my daddy stories about it, and my daddy has told me a few of them whenever we get a dust storm here. It was a horrible time for the people who lived in that area. High winds and dirt blew so badly they could hardly see or breathe."

"That's right," said Patch. "Their crops were wiped out, and it was a terrible time for those early settlers in the Texas Panhandle, Oklahoma, and surrounding states. That wind blew like crazy for so long that it made some people go crazy. It blew dust and dirt in the cracks around the doors and windows and left fine dust all over the house. Some people even got sick from dust pneumonia. Can you imagine having strong wind and dust beating up on you wherever you went day after day after day? Why, people had to tie a rope between the house and the barn to hang on to when they went back and forth. They were afraid they'd get blown away or get lost out in all that dirt and wind. There were times when they couldn't even see their hand right in front of their eyes.

"But, the worst day during that time was called Black Sunday. That was in April of 1935. There was a reporter visiting in the area. He was writin' a story about the drought and wind and blowing dirt, and he happened to witness the day known as Black Sunday. In his newspaper article, he named that period of time the Dust Bowl. From then on, that's what people called it."

"We have our own Dust Bowl out in that barn," said Dallas. "We stop from time to time and go outside to get some fresh air."

"Now, that's a smart thing to do," said Patch. "You don't want to get dust pneumonia."

The lunch break ended, and the ranch hands went back to work. The kids got back to their work in the old barn. By the end of the day, they each made a decision on what they would take to the campfire.

CHAPTER 10

CHUCK WAGONS, CATTLE TRAILS, AND CAPTAIN KING

MS. ADALINE asked Jennie's parents if she could spend one more night on the Double A Ranch while they made plans to bring little Jackson home from the hospital. They agreed, and Jennie was thrilled. She was becoming a part of the family on the Double A, and the boys actually enjoyed having her around.

After supper was eaten and cleaned up, Jennie and the boys gathered up the things they selected for the campfire. Hank also remembered to bring his binoculars. He put the strap of the binoculars on over his head. They had so many things to carry they decided to put them in the old red wagon and pull it over to the campfire.

"I used to be afraid of Patch," said Hank, "but not anymore. I like listening to him tell us stories."

Justin and Dallas smiled at each other as they remembered how Hank had been leery of Patch. It was a good lesson to all of them that you can't judge a book by its cover. On the outside, Patch looked tough and scary because of his bushy beard and toothless smile. Now that they knew him better, they realized he was kind, smart, a great storyteller, and a very nice cowboy.

The kids sat down around the campfire. Rowdy was playing a tune on his harmonica. Hank picked up the binoculars from around his neck and looked up at the moon and stars. Although they were far away, the stars were bright and twinkling in the clear summer sky. When Rowdy finished playing, he looked at the young cowpokes, and asked, "Did you bring some treasures for us to look at tonight?"

Hank jumped up and went to the wagon to get his treasure. It was obvious he wanted to be first. Hank came back to the fire with a small wooden car.

"I know what that is," said Rowdy. "Your daddy used to be a Cub Scout. He and Ace made that car for the Pinewood Derby. That was his first car, and he made another one the following year. He painted the second one black, and if I remember correctly, he won first place with it."

"Daddy made this?" asked Hank. He held it up to the light of the campfire and gave it a good look. "He did a pretty good job on it."

"Yep," said Patch. "He did a fine job on it. Ace made sure he did most of the work by himself. He worked hard on it. When he took it to the races, he noticed some other cars that must have been made by the fathers. Your daddy didn't care. The most important thing was to have the fastest car, and your daddy's car left those others in the dust."

"What else did y'all bring?" asked Rowdy.

Jennie wanted to be next, so she went to the wagon and got her treasure. She held it out so everyone could see it, and said, "Here's what I found. It's an old coffee pot."

"That old coffee pot is the one we once used on the chuck wagon," said Patch. He looked over at Slim, who had decided to join them at the campfire. Slim was not slim by any means. He stood about six feet tall and was a very large man. He had eaten plenty of good cooking in his days on the ranch, and it showed on his belly. Hank thought Slim was almost a twin to Santa Claus with his round belly and white beard.

"Yep," said Slim. "That one got so beat up we had to replace it. I've made a million cups of coffee in that old pot especially when we had the chuck wagon fired up. It was always hot and strong just the way we like it. I filled it with water and waited for it to boil. Next, I dumped in the coffee grounds, and let it boil for a while. Then right before I served it, I settled the coffee grounds down to the bottom of the pot by pouring in some cold water or ice. That coffee was so strong my spoon could stand up in it!"

"Now that's somethin' you need to see," said Patch, "our chuck wagon. What do you think, Slim? Do you think we could load it up for a good meal sometime soon?"

"Sure, we can," said Slim. "Just give me a few days to get everything together. I'll fix y'all a fine cowboy meal."

Slim told the boys that the chuck wagon was used on the cattle trail to prepare the meals for the cowboys. It carried all the pots, pans, supplies, and food the cowboys needed while they were out on the cattle trails. The cook prepared food that filled up the hungry men as they worked hard to move the cattle from the ranch to the market. The cook prepared biscuits and eggs for breakfast, and beans, chili, cornbread, and other one-pot meals for lunch and supper.

Rowdy stirred the campfire, and said, "Before the railroads were built, it took weeks to move the cattle from the ranches in Texas to the large cattle markets such as the one in Abilene, Kansas. When the railroads finally got to towns like Fort Worth, ranchers loaded the cattle on the trains and moved the cattle in railroad cars all the way to the market."

Rowdy continued, "There were several large ranches that became well-known in Texas. The most famous ranch in Texas is located in the Coastal Plains area of Texas, the King Ranch. It was started by Captain Richard King in 1853. Richard King was born in New York and left home as a teenager. He got a job on a boat and eventually became a captain on a steamboat on the Rio Grande.

"Captain King was a good business man, and he used his money to buy 15,500 acres of land in South Texas along the Santa Gerturdis Creek. He continued buying land, and when he died in 1885, he had a huge ranch of over 640,000 acres. His family went on buying land after he died, and at one time the King Ranch had 1.25 million acres of land. But, as family members died and the land was divided among the heirs, the size of the ranch changed. Today the ranch has 825,000 acres."

Rowdy poked the campfire with a stick to get the fire to burn a little higher, and then continued, "Patch and I used to go over to the

King Ranch when we were kids. We lived not far from there, and it was amazing to see what they had on the King Ranch. What I liked the most about it were all those Santa Gerturdis cattle and the cowboys. When Captain King first got his ranch, he hired cowboys from Mexico. They were called *Kineños*, or King's Men.

"One of these days," said Rowdy, "I hope you can visit the King Ranch. You'll see the King Ranch brand, the Running W, on all sorts of things down there. There is a museum and gift shop in Kingsville you'll want to stop in, and you might even want to buy yourself a new pair of boots from the King Ranch Saddle Shop."

Patch jumped into Rowdy's story with some information he thought was interesting. "There were lots of mighty fine cattlemen in early Texas," he said. "Some that come to my mind first are Charles Goodnight and Oliver Loving. Charles Goodnight was a cowboy, a Texas Ranger, and a wealthy cattle baron. He and his friend, Oliver Loving, were Texas pioneers who drove cattle from ranches to the cattle market. They worked as a team to forge the Goodnight-Loving Trail. Of course, they had some hired hands helping them. In fact, they had about eighteen cowboys working for them, and in June of 1866, they set out to blaze a trail from West Texas all the way to Wyoming. They moved 2,000 head of cattle out of Texas, and they made their first stop in Fort Sumner, New Mexico. From there, Oliver Loving went on to Denver with the cattle while Goodnight went back to West Texas for more."

Patch scratched his beard, and then continued his story, "That was a mighty dangerous cattle trail because the Indians didn't want those cowboys bringing cattle through their land. At one point, Oliver Loving was attacked by Comanches and seriously wounded.

It wasn't long before he died of his wounds. And you know what? Oliver Loving is buried right over there in Weatherford, Texas, not thirty miles from here.

"Ole Goodnight kept on drivin' cattle without Loving, but he got some help from another cowboy named John Simpson Chisum. Mr. Chisum was a wealthy cattle baron and had a large ranch in the Bosque Grande not too far from Fort Sumner, New Mexico. He formed a partnership with Goodnight and Loving to assemble and drive herds of cattle to sell to the U.S. Army in Fort Sumner and Santa Fe, New Mexico. They also planned to provide cattle to some miners in Colorado and the Bell Ranch.

"There was another cowboy that Charles Goodnight counted on," said Patch. "That would be his good and trusted friend, Bose Ikard. He is remembered as one of the best Black cowboys in history. Goodnight and Loving trusted him so much that they asked Ikard to carry the money after a successful cattle drive. Bose Ikard is buried in the same cemetery in Weatherford, Texas, that Oliver Loving is buried in."

"That's a cool story, Patch," said Dallas. "Cowboys had to depend on each other a lot back then, didn't they?"

"Yes, they did, Dallas," said Patch. "Even today we depend on each other. We work long and hard every day. Sometimes we get hurt or need help, and it sure is good to know there is always someone close by that you can count on."

"Now the name John Chisum reminds me of another cowboy. Have you heard of the Chisholm Trail?" asked Patch. "Jesse Chisholm was another great cowboy. He moved cattle on a different trail that became known as the Chisholm Trail. That cowboy moved cattle all the way from Brownsville, at the southern tip of Texas, to Abilene, Kansas. He'd pick up cattle along the way from other ranches so that he had thousands of cattle to deliver in Abilene when he finally got there."

As Patch finished his story about Jesse Chisholm, he began rubbing his left arm as if it were hurting him. He looked like he didn't feel well. He took off his cowboy hat and wiped his forehead with his kerchief. Rowdy noticed that Patch was not behaving his usual self, and asked him, "Patch, are you feelin' all right?"

"Naw, I'm not feeling too spunky," said Patch. "I think I'll say good night and head on in to the bunkhouse."

He got up slowly and started toward the bunkhouse. Slim got up at the same time and went with him to make sure he made it to the bunkhouse safely. It was the perfect example of one cowboy giving another cowboy a helping hand.

Rowdy watched Patch as he walked away. For the first time, he could see Patch as an old cowboy. All the years he had been out on the ranch were beginning to catch up with him. Rowdy hoped that Patch would be all right. Maybe he just needed a good night's sleep.

Dallas went over to the wagon and picked up his item for the campfire chat. He walked back with a shoe box. He took the lid off and showed some old fishing lures. He handed the box to Rowdy.

"Now, these will help you pull some fish out of Lake Granbury. Anybody here like to go fishin'?" asked Rowdy.

"Hank, Justin, and I do," said Dallas.

"Me, too," said Jennie. "I've got a brand new fishing pole that I've never used setting in my barn. Daddy bought it for me last year, but we haven't had a chance to use it yet."

"These lures have a treble hook on them," said Patch. "These are for catching some big fish, but I suppose all it takes is one hook to catch a fish. We could bait up all three hooks, throw the line into the water, and see what kind of fish nibbles on it. Why, we might even catch a whale out there!"

Hank laughed. Even he knew there weren't any whales in Lake Granbury. He asked Rowdy, "Are there any other places to fish around here?"

"There's Squaw Creek Lake over there by the nuclear plant. You head out like you're going to Glen Rose, and look for the sign. If it's open, you can pull some big bass out of that lake, but I haven't fished there in a while. They've had it closed to the public for quite some time. After the Twin Towers were destroyed in New York City on September 11, 2001, they shut Squaw Creek down to the public as a security measure. Squaw Creek Lake is right next to the nuclear plant, so they didn't want to let somebody that close to the plant that might want to do harm to the rest of us. Since then, the bass swimming around in the lake have grown bigger and bigger than ever before. Now, that would be a great place to go fishing! We just might need a big treble hook to pull in those bass!" said Rowdy with a smile.

There was still one more item to talk about. Justin had not had the opportunity to show off his treasure yet. He went to the wagon and pulled out an old pair of spurs. He held them out for Rowdy to look over.

"Now those are some mighty fine spurs you got there," said Rowdy. He looked closely at the spurs, and then said, "You found some lady leg spurs, Justin. Did you notice this part right here looks like a lady's leg?"

"Yes, sir," said Justin. "Are those for women or men?"

"These could be for either one, but I bet these were either your daddy's or granddaddy's spurs," said Rowdy. "Cowboys use these to nudge their horses to get them to move faster. Cowboys don't use them often, but there are times when you need to git someplace in a hurry or move fast to git to a runaway cow or calf. Moving cattle from one place to another can be tricky. The cattle can be moving along just fine and if for some reason they get spooked, they are likely to take off in all directions. That's when a cowboy earns his wages. He has to git movin' fast to settle the herd down and keep them all going in the same direction."

With Patch gone, the campfire seemed quiet. Everyone decided to call it a night. Rowdy stood up first, and said, "Thank you for your company tonight, but this cowboy is going inside. I want to check on Patch. Good night, young cowpokes. I'll see you in the morning."

Jennie and the boys walked back to the Main House with Hank pulling the wagon. As they walked, they talked about going someplace fun like Fossil Rim Wildlife Center in Glen Rose. Jennie said, "It's a lot of fun. We went there last year and saw all of the animals. We even had a picnic out there. Maybe if we helped pay our own way we could get Ace and Ms. Adaline to take us."

Photo by Nancy Sifford Alana

Fossil Rim Wildlife Center, Glen Rose, TX

"That's a great idea," said Dallas, "but how are we going to earn some money?"

"What about trying to sell some of that stuff in the barn? We could have a barn sale. I bet we could make a lot of money and help clear out some of that stuff in the junk barn."

"That's a great idea," said Hank, "but there's some of this stuff I don't want to sell. I don't want to sell my wagon."

"We don't have to sell everything, silly," said Justin. "We'll need to talk with Ace and Ms. Adaline to see what we can sell. These things belong to them, so we have to have their permission before we do anything. Besides, it's going to take a lot of work to have a barn sale, and we will need their help. Is everyone ready to work in order to make it happen?"

With excitement, they all told Justin they were willing to do it. In order to get it all together, it was going to take some planning, and they were willing to do just that.

"Come on," said Hank as he took off running with the wagon bouncing behind him. "Let's go ask Ace."

CHAPTER 11
PLANNING A BARN SALE

JENNIE AND THE BOYS burst through the front doors of the Main House. Ace and Ms. Adaline were sitting at the kitchen table sipping a cup of coffee and eating a slice of apple pie.

"Ace, we want to have a barn sale," said Dallas.

"Well, that sounds good, but I don't have any barns for sale," said Ace. "I think you need to slow down and tell me what's on your mind, cowboy."

"We don't want to sell your barn," laughed Justin. "We'd like to make some money while we are here, and we thought if we sold some of the junk in the barn, we would have enough money to do something. Would that be all right with you?"

"Do something special?" asked Ace. "Now, just what kind of special thing do you have in mind?"

"We'd like to go to Fossil Rim Wildlife Center," said Dallas. "Jennie said it's a lot of fun, and we could have a picnic while we are there if Ms. Adaline didn't mind making one for us." Dallas looked over at Ms. Adaline and smiled a sweet smile trying to be irresistible. It must have worked.

"I don't see why not," said Ms. Adaline. "I love picnics, and we need to get rid of some of that junk. Don't we, Ace?" She looked at Ace hoping he'd agree with her. She'd been trying to clean some of that junk out of the barn for years.

"I think that would be just fine," said Ace. "I need to help you sort out some of that junk, though. I don't want you puttin' my good stuff up for sale. When do you want to do this?"

Justin spoke up for the group. "What do you think about next Friday? That will give us a week to get it all together. We'll get started planning right now, and we'll come back to you with what we'd like to do."

"Well, you get busy with your plan, come back in here, and then we'll talk about it," said Ace.

Jennie and the boys went into the living room so they could talk about what they wanted to do. Justin asked Dallas to get his spiral notebook and pencil. Dallas returned to the group ready to write down their plans.

"Here's what I think," said Justin. "I think we should bring everything we want to sell outside of the barn, clean it up, and put a price tag on it."

"That's good," said Hank. "I like that idea." Justin smiled at Hank. It pleased Justin to see Hank eager to help out and do his part.

"I agree," said Dallas. "That's a good idea, but how are we going to get people to stop and buy the stuff?"

"That's what I can do," said Jennie. "I'll get some poster boards and make some signs to put by the road. I'll even get some balloons to put on the signs. People driving by will see the signs and stop to look at our stuff."

"That's good, Jennie," said Justin. "I have my camera, and we can take some pictures of the best items and make some flyers to hand-out to people on the Square."

"That's a great idea," said Jennie. "My dad can help us make the flyers. He does all kinds of things like that on the computer."

"Maybe he can e-mail all his friends about it, too," said Dallas.

"Sure, he can do that," said Jennie. "I think he would be happy to do that for us."

"Now, what day do we want to do this?" asked Dallas.

"You mentioned Friday to Ace. I think that would be a great day." said Jennie. "That will give us six days to get everything ready and get the word out."

"Great," said Justin. "Dallas, did you get all of that?"

Dallas nodded his head, stood up, and started back into the kitchen where Ace and Ms. Adaline were still talking.

"We've got a plan," said Dallas. He read off the details of the plan he had written down. Ace listened closely, nodded, and then said, "Sounds like a good plan to me. Ms. Adaline and I were just talking about it, and we can help you out some. I'll help you sort through that stuff and tell you what you can sell. Ms. Adaline will help you get a money box ready so that you can make change. She'll stay close by to keep an eye on the money box and help you out if you have any questions."

"That would be great," said Jennie. "We knew we could count on you to help us. You are the best neighbors anyone could ever hope for."

"Well, that's enough thinking and planning for one day," said Ace. "It's time to hit the hay. Good night, sleep tight, and don't let the bed bugs bite." Ace stood up and headed to his bedroom.

"Boys, before you go to bed, I need for you to gather up all your dirty clothes," said Ms. Adaline. "I need to wash them up in the morning."

"Hank," said Justin. "Go get your Spiderman underwear."

"I smelled *your* stinky underwear from across the room last night," said Hank.

"Now, now, boys," said Ms. Adaline. "High-tail it into the Cowboy Room and get your stinky underwear and all the other dirty clothes you've got hidden in there."

Jennie laughed at all of them. She hoped she and her little brother would have a good time teasing one another one of these days.

"All right, Miss Jennie," said Ms. Adaline. "Let's get your bed ready while those boys gather up their dirty clothes."

Ms. Adaline helped Jennie get her sleeping place ready on the sofa. After everyone was in bed, Ms. Adaline turned out the lights and went to bed.

Even though they were in bed, their minds were still spinning. The plans had been finalized, but they could hardly wait until the next morning. The boys hoped Jennie would be able to stay long enough the next day to help them out. There were many things to go through in the barn, but they would have plenty of time before the sale.

Dallas tossed and turned in his bed. There was a lot on his mind. Along with the barn sale, he couldn't get Patch off his mind. He hoped Patch was feeling better.

CHAPTER 12

PATCH'S UNEXPECTED RIDE

RIGHT AFTER BREAKFAST, Jennie and the boys headed to the barn. They each put a kerchief in their back pocket in case they needed it. All the dust in the air had caused several sneezing attacks while they had been digging through the junk. On their way to the barn, they stopped long enough at the bunkhouse to let Rowdy know where they were going and what they were going to do. Rowdy thought the barn sale was an excellent idea.

Justin opened the doors to the barn and propped them open with some old boards that were stacked beside the barn. Ace wasn't too far behind them. He stuck his head in the barn, and said, "Look at all this junk!" He rubbed his hands together. "Okay, Justin, what's the plan?"

"We thought we would take the stuff outside the barn that we want to sell. That way we can clean it up and make room in the barn so that we can get to the other stuff," said Justin.

"Great idea," said Ace. "Let's start with this old chair. Justin and Dallas, you ought to be able to carry it outside. Y'all stay close to me, and I'll point out things that you can sell."

They all worked hard moving and sorting. The items moved outside were beginning to add up. They felt confident they would be able to make enough money to go to Fossil Rim.

Jennie went back to the Main House and got some cleaning supplies from Ms. Adaline. She was going to start dusting and cleaning up the items. Justin came out with his camera and took some pictures of the some of the items. He planned to give the digital card to Jennie so her dad could make some flyers to hand out.

Everyone was working away when they heard some of the cowboys shouting. Ace looked up from what he was doing, and said, "Let me go check on those cowboys and see what's going on. Y'all stay in here."

Jennie and the boys kept on working. Dallas found a U. S. flag on a wooden pole and brought it out into the sunshine. He found a good place for it so that it didn't touch the ground. While he was doing that, he thought he caught a glimpse of something run up a tree close by. He approached the tree slowly and kept his eye out for it. He hoped it was only a lizard and not something else. Ace had told him to watch out for snakes. Rattlesnakes were all over the ranch, and he had learned a long time ago to stay out of the tall grass. He tip-toed over to the tree and spotted an odd looking lizard.

"Justin!" Dallas yelled. "Come here! Look at this lizard!"

Justin came running. He slowed down right before he got there and tip-toed to where Dallas was standing. "Look at it," said Dallas, pointing to the spot on the tree where the lizard had stopped in its tracks, not moving or even blinking his eyes. "Right there on the tree."

"That's one of those horned toads I was telling you about," said Justin. "Be careful. He won't bite you, but he might shoot blood at you."

"You're kidding me, right?" asked Dallas.

"No, I'm not kidding," said Justin. "They shoot blood out of their eyes at their enemies. It won't hurt you. It just looks bad."

Jennie and Hank came running over behind Justin. They wanted to see the odd-looking lizard, too. Jennie said, "Oh, that's just a horned toad. My dad calls them horned frogs, but that's because he went to TCU, and that's their mascot. They won't hurt you. In fact, they are good for the environment. You should just let it go."

"I think it's cool that the mascot for TCU is a horned frog!" laughed Hank.

"This is the sign they use to represent the horned frogs," said Jennie. She held up her right hand with her index and middle fingers curled under. "When we go to TCU games, we use this sign to show our support for the team. Did you know that TCU got its start in Hood County?"

"No way," said Dallas. "TCU started in Hood County?"

"My dad said that it was called Add-Ran College and was located in Thorp Spring. He said that years later it was moved to Waco because of some problems. Then, there was a fire in the building in Waco. Instead of rebuilding it, they moved it to Fort Worth. That's when the name was changed to Texas Christian University."

"Where is Thorp Spring?" asked Hank.

"Thorp Spring is a small community just north of Granbury," said Jennie. "Dad took me out there one time. There is a historical marker that tells all about it. They had several buildings out there including dorms for the boys and girls to live in."

"Wow," said Justin. "That's interesting. Why did they choose the horned frog to be their mascot?"

"My dad told me about it," said Jennie. "He said when TCU was being built horned frogs were all over the ground where the football field is now. Someone suggested it be their mascot. I guess everyone else thought it was a good idea, too."

All of a sudden, they heard a siren. They looked up and saw an ambulance coming down the road. It pulled in the main entrance and headed toward the bunkhouse. They ran over to the bunkhouse to see what was going on. Ms. Adaline was already there and told them to stay back out of the way. Even though they did as she asked, they could see someone on a stretcher being loaded into the ambulance. It was Patch.

They couldn't say a word to each other. They exchanged looks of disbelief. Ms. Adaline finally spoke up, "Now, don't you worry about Patch. Ace said he should be just fine. He wasn't feeling good this morning, and Ace told Rowdy to take him to the doctor. When Patch tried to stand up, he felt some pain in his chest and his legs gave out from under him. They decided it was better to get an ambulance here rather than having Rowdy drive him in. That way the paramedics would be on hand in case he got worse. They'll get him to the hospital in Granbury quicker than we can."

Tears welled up in everyone's eyes as the ambulance pulled away with Patch inside.

"Come on, now," said Ms. Adaline. "Let's go inside. I need to make some lunch for us. I think it's a good day to bake some chocolate chip cookies for an afternoon snack. What do y'all think?"

"Ms. Adaline, it's always a good day for your chocolate chip cookies," said Justin.

Ms. Adaline smiled. Chocolate chip cookies were her idea of comfort food.

CHAPTER 13
ACE'S PROMISE

NOT TOO LONG after being admitted to the hospital, Patch was moved to a private room. He was already showing improvement, but he needed to spend more time in the hospital so the doctors could run some tests to determine what was wrong with his heart.

Jennie's parents came by the Double A on their way home from the hospital to pick up Jennie. They were anxious to have their whole family together at home. Jackson Christopher was strapped into the car seat and fast asleep. Jennie got in the back seat and sat next to him. She smiled at how tiny he was. She could hardly wait to hold him for the first time. Jennie knew she was going to enjoy being a big sister to young Mr. Jackson Christopher Dilka.

The boys did not feel like looking through the barn anymore after seeing Patch leave in the ambulance. Ms. Adaline made some lunch for them. After lunch, she made a batch of chocolate chip cookies, just as she promised. The boys stayed in the Main House for the remainder of the day. They didn't want to get too far away from the phone in case Ace called with information about Patch. They found some board games in the closet and spent their time playing Monopoly, Clue, and Yahtzee. They even pulled out Ace's arrowhead collection so Hank could see what an arrowhead looked like.

Just like clockwork, Ace showed up at the Double A Ranch just in time for supper. He looked tired and weary, but he assured everyone that Patch was going to be fine. He might have to take it easy for a while, but with some medication and changes in his diet, he should be just fine.

"This is a good reminder to all of us that we need to take better care of ourselves," said Ms. Adaline. "Perhaps we need to go on a diet and stop eating so many desserts around here."

Ace sure did hate to hear that. "Now, Ms. Adaline, let's don't get carried away. Although we probably do need to make some changes, you know it's going to be hard on this ole cowboy. I've enjoyed your good cookin' for over forty years now, and I can't hardly imagine not havin' my dessert at the end of a good meal."

"Ace, you need to take better care of yourself, or you're going to end up in the hospital just like Patch," said Ms. Adaline.

"Come on, Ace, you can do anything you want to do. I don't want you to be in the hospital like Patch," said Hank. He left his chair at the supper table and walked down to stand by Ace. Hank crawled up on Ace's lap. The boys had a hard time imagining Ace in the hospital especially after seeing Patch leave the ranch in an ambulance.

"All right, boys, I get it," said Ace. "I promise to take better care of myself."

That night when the boys went to bed, they said a special prayer for Patch. They hoped they would be able to go see him in the hospital, but Ace said it would have to wait until Monday. Patch needed to rest for a couple of days before having any visitors. It was going to be a long week-end unless they found something to keep their minds off of Patch.

Ms. Adaline stopped by the Cowboy Room before she went to bed. "Boys, let's go to the Square in Granbury tomorrow. How about that?"

"That would be great, Ms. Adaline!" said Hank.

Ms. Adaline gave him a wink as she turned to go to bed. "Get a good night's sleep, boys," she said. "Tomorrow will be a busy day!"

Ms. Adaline had a way of knowing what those boys needed.

CHAPTER 14

LEGENDS AND HISTORY OF HOOD COUNTY

BRIGHT AND EARLY on Saturday morning, Rowdy stopped by the Main House to get Ace. They drove into Granbury to go spend some time with Patch at the hospital. Ms. Adaline promised to take the boys to the historic town square in Granbury. The locals referred to it as the "Square." Standing in the middle of the Square is the Hood County Courthouse that was built in 1891. Today, on the four sides of the Square are stores of all kinds just as it was when Hood County was beginning to be established.

In the early days of Hood County and most other counties in Texas, the streets around the courthouse were made of dirt. People came into town on horseback or in wagons to take care of business, buy food and supplies, and visit with other people from around the county. The businesses in early Texas towns included dry good stores, restaurants, banks, and grocery stores. Most towns also had a barber shop and drug store. Some towns like Granbury even had an Opera House where live theater and music were performed by local entertainers. There was usually a checker game going on with some older men somewhere on the courthouse lawn. It was a gathering place for people to socialize and take care of business and shopping needs.

Photo by Nancy Sifford Alana

The Hood County Courthouse was built in 1891.

The boys loved to look at the old jail in Granbury even though it was somewhat frightening to them. The old jail is catty-cornered from the Hood County Courthouse. It was built in 1885 and is a museum today. After prisoners were booked into the jail at the courthouse, they were escorted to the jail by the sheriff or jailer.

Photo by Nancy Sifford Alana

The old Hood County Jail is now a museum.

Photo by Nancy Sifford Alana

Nutt House Hotel was built in 1893 and was originally a mercantile building.

The cell block that housed the prisoners was located up a narrow set of stairs. The prisoners were held securely in the cell by a steel-plated lattice door. The most intriguing part of the jail was the gallows where prisoners could be hung. In all the years the jail housed prisoners, no one was ever hung.

The first floor of the jail had three rooms which were used by the sheriff or the jailer who lived there. The wife of the sheriff or jailer had to do all the cooking for the prisoners. The prisoners were fed two meals a day.

As the boys walked back to the Square after visiting the old jail, they saw the Nutt House. It was built in 1893 and was originally a mercantile building. It was owned by Jesse F. and Jacob Nutt. They were brothers, and both of them were blind.

In the late 1960s, Mary Lou Watkins and her cousin, Joe Nutt, restored the mercantile building and turned it into the Nutt House Restaurant. A statue of Mary Lou Watkins is located on the corner across the street from the Nutt House building. The statue shows her ringing a dinner bell just as she used to do to let everyone know that a home-cooked dinner was being served at the Nutt House Restaurant.

Today, the Nutt House has a store downstairs, and the upstairs portion of the building has living quarters with rooms that can be rented by visitors. In whatever way the building is used, it remains a historic building that is admired by everyone who enters it.

The boys loved to hear the stories about Granbury. They especially enjoyed hearing the ones about two famous citizens of Granbury. Those two famous men were said to be running from the law and hiding out in Granbury. They were Jesse James and John Wilkes Booth.

There is a headstone in the City of Granbury Cemetery for Jesse Woodson James. It shows that he was born in 1847 and died in 1951. While most people believe Jesse James was killed in St. Joseph, Missouri, many people in Granbury believe that he escaped and settled in Granbury.

In 1951, J. Frank Dalton became very ill and asked to be brought to Granbury in an ambulance. It was then that he told everyone he was really Jesse James. He lived with the local constable, Sam Rash, while he was on his death bed. People paid twenty-five cents to go in and see him. He died on August 15, 1951.

Photo by Nancy Sifford Alana

The statue of Mary Lou Watkins stands on the corner across the street from the Nutt House Hotel.

It is uncertain if J. Frank Dalton was the real Jesse James. In the 1990s, several of Jesse James' great-grandsons came to Granbury. They believed that their great-grandfather was buried in Granbury based on family stories and what they remembered about him. In fact, what was believed to be his body was exhumed from the City of Granbury Cemetery after his great-grandsons came to Granbury.

They were hoping to find some DNA to test, but when they brought up the body, it was the body of a one-armed man and not Jesse James. The legal process to exhume a body is difficult and time consuming, and another body was not exhumed. As a result, the mystery continues to this day.

There is another Hood County legend. John Wilkes Booth, the man who shot President Abraham Lincoln, is believed by most historians to have been killed in Port Royal, Virginia, where he was hiding in a barn suffering from a broken leg. The barn he was hiding in was set on fire, and a body was recovered after the barn burned to the ground. The body was said to be that of John Wilkes Booth. Granbury legend says that John Wilkes Booth escaped from the burning barn and went to Glen Rose. He left Glen Rose and moved to Granbury using the name John St. Helen. He was an actor, just as Booth was, and he walked with a limp as if his leg had been broken and not cared for properly. He never told anyone he was John Wilkes Booth until he became very ill. He thought he was going to die, and he confessed to F. J. Gordon and a Catholic priest from Dallas that he was John Wilkes Booth and had shot President Lincoln. Mr. Gordon went to St. Helen's home and found a derringer wrapped in a newspaper that told of the death of Lincoln. St. Helen said he used the gun to shoot Lincoln and told Mr. Gordon to keep it. Much to his own surprise, St. Helen recovered from his illness. Since he confessed to killing Lincoln, he decided he needed to leave Granbury.

In 1903, a house painter in Enid, Oklahoma, named David George died, but before he died he confessed that he was John Wilkes Booth and John St. Helen of Granbury. It remains a mystery whether John St. Helen was in fact the legendary John Wilkes Booth.

Ms. Adaline and the boys were hot and tired after their tour around town. They decided to stop by for some ice cream at Rinky Tinks, the local ice cream parlor on the Square. Bob and Jo Ann Skelton greeted the boys with big smiles and friendly conversation. They were the kind of hard-working, friendly people that have made Granbury a great place to live for many years. The boys loved to stop in at Rinky Tinks whenever they visited in Hood County.

The boys and Ms. Adaline sat on the swivel stools at the counter and ate their ice cream. Bob played a couple of songs from the 50s and 60s on the piano and invited the boys to sing along with him. Bob had been a recording artist in the 1960s and was an excellent musician. He went by the name of Bobby Skel when he wrote and recorded his music. The boys felt honored to sing along with him.

Jo Ann loved seeing the boys having a good time in Rinky Tinks. She gave each of the boys a quarter to use in the juke box. After the boys heard the songs they selected, they gave Bob and Jo Ann a hug and said good-bye. They loaded up in Ms. Adaline's Suburban to head back to the Double A. They still had time to do some exploring out on the ranch.

CHAPTER 15
CHESTER

MS. ADALINE prepared supper for everyone while the boys played outside. One of the best things about being at the ranch was that no one watched television or played video games. It motivated everyone to read, play board games, or go outside and find something to do.

The boys started walking toward the old barn when Hank spotted the rooster. Ms. Adaline kept a few chickens and one rooster on the ranch. She liked to gather fresh eggs every day. She swore they tasted better than store-bought eggs.

The rooster was named Chester. He was mean and didn't want anyone messing with the hens. He protected the hens by flying into the air and flapping his wings to scare away any man or beast who he thought was a threat.

The boys decided to sneak up on Chester and scare him before he had a chance to attack them. The boys walked quietly on their tip-toes until they were right behind Chester. Then they started yelling and waving their arms. Chester flapped his wings, squawked, and flew in the air a short distance. The boys started laughing at Chester, and he stopped long enough to turn around and look at what startled him. He eyed the boys for a couple of seconds, puffed out his feathers so he looked twice his normal size, flapped his wings, and began the chase that should have been captured on video. Chester was a very angry rooster, and he wasn't going to let the boys have the last word. The boys ran around in circles screaming as Chester charged at whoever was the closest to him.

After a few seconds of squawking and flapping, Hank had had enough. He took off running to the bunkhouse with Justin and Dallas right behind him screaming as they ran. Once they were safe on the porch, they laughed so hard they had tears running down their faces.

"Hank, you should have seen your face!" laughed Justin.

"He scared the dickens out of me!" said Hank. "I thought he was going to get me for sure!"

Dallas continued laughing and wiping the tears from his eyes. "Did you see how big he puffed up? He scared me, too, Hank!"

Slim stepped out of the bunkhouse to see what all the commotion was about. "I thought we had some girls out here," said Slim. "I haven't heard that much screaming since Ace put his ugly bare foot on a bed of fire ants!"

"We were running away from Chester before he shredded us to pieces," said Justin. "He's a mean rooster, Slim. Why is he so mean?"

"He is the guard of the hen house. His job is to protect his hens, and that's serious business to ole Chester," said Slim.

"Did you say Ace was dancing barefooted on an ant bed?" asked Dallas. The boys laughed at the thought of Ace dancing from one foot to the other while he was barefooted on a bed of angry fire ants.

"It was the funniest sight I've ever seen!" said Slim. "A couple of fire ants got down in his sock, so he stopped and took off his boot and sock. When he put his foot down, he wasn't lookin' at what he was doing. He put that ugly foot of his smack-dab in the middle of a mess of ants. They were moving around fast and bitin' whatever they could sink their biters into. He was slappin' his legs and feet all over the place! Poor Ace was dancin' like a cat on a hot tin roof!"

Once again they all laughed so hard, they had tears rolling down their cheeks. It felt good to laugh hard. They all needed it after all the worrying they had been doing over Patch.

After the boys finally stopped laughing, they sat down on the front porch of the bunkhouse and visited with Slim. The boys told him about all the things they did while they were in town.

"Looky who's coming down the road!" said Slim. It was Ace and Rowdy coming in from the hospital.

The boys took off running to the Main House to greet them. Ace opened the passenger side of Rowdy's pickup and slowly stepped out. "Did you boys have a good day?" asked Ace.

"Yes, sir," said Justin. "Ms. Adaline took us into Granbury. We saw the old jail again. We stopped in at Rinky Tinks and most of the stores on the Square. Ms. Adaline's in the house fixing supper for us right now."

"That's good 'cause I'm hungry enough to eat a horse," said Ace. He waved good-bye to Rowdy and put his arms around the boys. "Come on, cowboys. Let's go see what Ms. Adaline is cookin' up for supper."

Ace told Ms. Adaline, "It's a good thing Rowdy and I were at the hospital today with Patch. He was as ornery as all get out today. Nurse Lucas asked him to take his medicine, and he shut his mouth tight just like a little kid. Finally, she told him he could have some ice cream if he'd just take his medicine. You should have seen that mouth fly open!" The boys laughed at the thought of Patch acting like a kid.

Ace laughed and said, "Then Patch didn't like his dinner. He said he didn't like the food in the hospital so he wasn't going to eat anything. Rowdy looked his food over, and then he took a bite of the mashed potatoes. That's when Patch yelled at him, and told him to git away from his food. *Now*, he was ready to eat. He ate every last bite. There wasn't anything wrong with that food. He just acted like a whinny baby."

"Well, the boys and I had a wonderful day in Granbury," said Ms. Adaline. "We went through the old jail again, and we went to Rinky Tinks and some of the stores on the Square. We saw the statue of Mary Lou Watkins across from the Nutt House, and we read all the historical markers around the Square."

"It sounds like you boys have had a busy day," said Ace. "What have you been doing since you got home?"

The boys shared their story about Chester. They acted out the story to show Ace how they tip-toed up behind Chester to scare him. Ace laughed and laughed with the boys. He laughed so hard he cried, and he had to get out his kerchief to blow his nose! He got a kick out the boys having fun times on the ranch. He knew fun times like these would create some special memories for them as they got older.

"Ace," asked Justin as he looked at Hank and Dallas with a smile on his face. "Have you ever danced on an ant bed with your bare feet?"

"Now, who told you about that?" asked Ace. He tried to look angry, but the boys knew he wasn't. "Did Slim tell you that story? Well, that old goat!"

They all sat down around the supper table to enjoy Ms. Adaline's home-cooked meal of fried chicken, mashed potatoes, fresh black-eyed peas, and fried okra. Ms. Adaline served slices of a sweet watermelon for dessert.

After supper, the boys helped Ms. Adaline to clear the table, clean up the kitchen, and take out the trash. Instead of going to the campfire, they decided to stay in and look at some old photo albums Ms. Adaline had pulled out of the closet. They laughed at the old pictures of their dad when he was a little boy, but they the laughed the hardest of all at Ms. Adaline's hair styles over the years. She laughed, too, and wondered why she ever wore her hair in those styles.

It had been a great day for the boys, and they were now exhausted. With "good nights" shared all around, the boys put on their pajamas while Ace headed for bed.

Ms. Adaline checked on the boys before she turned out the lights. She smiled as she thought about how blessed they were to have such wonderful grandsons who enjoyed spending time with them during the summer. She knew that time would march on, and one of these days the boys would grow up and have families of their own. That's the great thing about families. They pass down to the next generation their memories and traditions. Even though life ends in one way, it continues on in many other.

Ms. Adaline went to the bedside of each of the boys and gave them a kiss on their foreheads and straightened their covers. She thought they were asleep, but they weren't. They smiled when she left the room, and snuggled in for a good night's sleep.

CHAPTER 16
COWBOY CHURCH

SUNDAY MORNING was quiet at the ranch. It was customary for the cowboys on the Double A to get together in the bunkhouse for Cowboy Church on Sunday morning. Ace and Ms. Adaline usually walked over to join the cowboys as they sang hymns, heard an inspirational talk, and had a time of prayer.

The boys put on a clean pair of starched jeans along with a nice shirt. Dallas asked Ace if he could borrow a bolo tie to wear to church. A bolo tie is worn by some cowboys instead of a regular neck tie. It is a cord with metal tips that goes around the neck like a tie. It has a decorative slide on it to hold the strings together.

The cowboys were all dressed up in their Sunday shirts and jeans. They were sitting at the tables waiting for the service to begin. Ace, Ms. Adaline, and the boys found a place at one of the tables.

Slim welcomed everyone and led the singing. They sang "Amazing Grace" and "The Old Rugged Cross" while one of the cowboys played the guitar, and Rowdy played the harmonica.

After the singing, Rowdy got up and read a passage from the Bible. He began speaking, and the boys listened closely to every word. "This morning we are missing one of our own. As you know, Patch is in the hospital in Granbury. We are thankful that he is doing much better today, but we still need to pray for that old cowboy." After a short pause he said, "And you might want to pray for his nurses, too!" Everyone laughed. They had already heard Patch was being ornery.

Rowdy continued, "I won't keep you long this morning, but since I had a chance this week to do some thinking while sitting in Patch's room, I thought I'd share with you some of those thoughts. One of the hardest things to see in life is one of your brothers loaded into an ambulance. Now, Patch and I are not blood brothers, but there is no doubt that we are family. I've known Patch almost all of my life. I've seen him at his best, and I've seen him at his worst.

"I consider all of you to be my family, too. We work together almost every day. We have fun together while we live and work together. There are also times we celebrate together. Why, even though we are tough cowboys, we even cry together sometimes. When one of us is sick or hurt, we look out for each other. Now, this ole world is a mighty fine place with all the beauty around us. Just look out here at the Double A Ranch at all the beauty. Even that ole bull in the pasture is a beautiful work of art. In the spring, we admire the wildflowers and the awakening of the trees and flowers as they bloom after a cold winter. In the summer, we appreciate the cool waters that flow continuously from the spring in the creek, the clear blue skies, and the sweet watermelons that grow in the sunshine. In the fall, we appreciate the changing colors on the trees and the cool mornings and the warm afternoons. And, in the winter, we bundle up in our cold gear for the occasional ice and snow that covers the land with a blanket of frosty white.

"All year long we are blessed when the newborn calves are born. We are blessed when we load up the cattle to send to them to market. We are blessed to have Ace and Ms. Adaline as our bosses, mentors, and friends. We are also blessed each summer to have Justin, Dallas, and Hank join us and remind us that what we do out here every day makes for a great life whether you are two or a hundred and two.

"I bet Patch is wishin' he was here his morning, and if all goes well, he will be here next Sunday mornin'. If he were here, he'd tell you he was thankful for the doctors, nurses, and his ranch family that are with him in good times and bad. On the other hand, he would also tell you that he was given a good reminder this week that our time on this earth is not gonna last forever. Just as the flowers bloom in the spring, they also wither away. Everything that is born is going to die at some time. If that time for Patch had been a couple of days ago, Patch would have wanted us to celebrate all the good has done in his life, not sit around and cry about him being gone. So prepare yourselves right now. One of these days you *will* say good-bye to Patch and to everyone else in this room. One of these days, we will all say good-bye to you.

"I hope as you leave here today you will remember you are never promised that tomorrow will be here for you. Be good to one another and to all people you meet today. Do good things for one another and for people you may not even know. When you git up in the mornin', you should be thankful for another day to be productive and do good things. I know Patch is thankful for another day to live and work. We should all live as if today were our last. I hope this will give you something to think about this week."

With that, Rowdy sat down. Slim led the group in the song, "Walking in Sunlight." When the song ended, everyone spent some time visiting with one another while Slim got dinner ready to serve.

Ace went over to Rowdy and shook his hand, "I enjoyed your message today, Rowdy. You gave us some good things to think about."

Rowdy said, "Thank you, Ace. I'm gonna run into town in a bit to see Patch. Do you want to go with me?"

"Yes, I'd like to go. Let's get some dinner before we head out," said Ace.

Slim set out a dinner that Patch would have loved: barbecue brisket, corn on the cob, fresh green beans, hot rolls, and sweet tea. After blessing the food, Slim said, "Let's eat!"

The boys loaded up their plates. They found a place at the table to eat with Ace and Ms. Adaline. Ace asked the boys, "What are you boys going to do this afternoon?"

Justin said, "We haven't talked about it yet, but I was wondering if we could go over to Jennie's ranch. She told us she owned a horse for barrel racing. I was hoping we could watch her ride."

"I don't think that will be a problem," said Ms. Adaline. "I'll call over there after dinner and see if it would be all right. I would like to see if there is anything I can do to help her mother now that Mr. Jackson Christopher Dilka is home."

The boys smiled at each other. Despite the fact that Jennie was a girl, she was now a good friend to the boys.

CHAPTER 17
JENNIE AND GYPSY

MS. ADALINE asked the boys to help her load up the food that she was going to take over to Jennie's house. She made chicken and dumplings and her famous sauerkraut cake for the Dilka family to enjoy. She hoped it would help them out. By not having to cook anything for supper, Mrs. Dilka could rest or spend time with her family, and it was the proper thing to do in Texas for neighbors.

Ms. Adaline and the boys headed down the road to the Dilka Ranch. The boys held onto the food so it wouldn't turn over. It smelled delicious, and the boys had a hard time not sneaking a taste of the chocolate icing on the cake.

Mr. and Mrs. Dilka were in their house when Ms. Adaline pulled into the circular driveway. As soon as Mr. Dilka heard the doors to the Suburban close, he came outside to help bring in the food and to welcome his visitors. Jennie was not far behind him.

The boys smiled when they saw her. They entered the house and went straight into the kitchen with the food.

"I heard Patch is still in the hospital," said Jennie. "Is that true?" Jennie had known Patch all of her life, and she was genuinely concerned about him.

"Ace said that he is going to be fine. We want to go see him tomorrow in the hospital. Do you want to go with us?" asked Justin.

"Sure," said Jennie. "Dad, can I?"

"That would be a good thing for you to do as long as you behave yourself and don't get in the way. A hospital is no place for messing around," said Mr. Dilka.

"They'll be fine. I'll watch them like a hawk," said Ms. Adaline. "Patch could use someone to lift his spirits."

"Where's your little brother?" asked Hank.

"He's in his cradle over there, but he's sleeping right now. He sleeps a lot. We've decided to call him J. C.," said Jennie as she led the boys into the den to show off her new little brother.

"He's awfully little," said Dallas.

"Yes, he is," said Ms. Adaline. Everyone could tell she wanted to pick him up and hold him, but she would have to wait until he woke up. She knew better than to disturb a sleeping baby.

Mrs. Dilka came into the den to welcome her guests. "Something smells delicious! Ms. Adaline, I hope you didn't go to a lot of trouble."

"Why, I just brought over some chicken and dumplings and some chocolate cake for your family," Ms. Adaline said. She didn't tell her it was a sauerkraut cake, and the boys smiled. "Now, I'm going to skedaddle before I wake up little J. C. I'll come back later and pick up the boys. Now, you boys behave yourselves, and don't wake up the baby."

"Yes, ma'am, we will be good," said Dallas.

Ms. Adaline returned to the Double A, and Jennie and the boys headed outside. She wanted to show them her horse, Gypsy, and the riding arena. Mr. Dilka built an arena where she could practice barrel racing. She looked at barrel racing as if it were a team sport. In order to be a winner, she and Gypsy had to work together as if they were one. In order for them to do that, they had to practice a lot. Jennie was committed to being the best barrel racer in the whole state of Texas one day.

Jennie led the boys to the horse barn. Gypsy was a beautiful and unusual blue roan. She was barely 15 hands tall and was the quickest horse ever seen in Hood County. Her body looked more like a red roan, but she had a black mane and tail and was considered a blue roan. She was absolutely beautiful and stunning when she entered into the arena.

It was Jennie's responsibility to take care of Gypsy, and she loved every minute of it. She required almost as much attention from Jennie as little J. C. did from Mrs. Dilka. Gypsy had to be fed, watered, exercised, curried, and combed every day. Jennie also had the responsibility to muck her stall. If for some reason Jennie or her dad wasn't able to tend to Gypsy, they had to ask one of the ranch hands to help them out.

The boys watched Jennie put the tack on Gypsy like an expert. Tack is the equipment used on a horse. To get Gypsy ready, Jennie put the bridle, saddle blanket, and barrel saddle on her. A barrel saddle has shorter flaps on the back of the saddle that allow Gypsy to have full use and motion of her back as she turns around the barrels.

Jennie also needed to be properly dressed for riding. She had on Wrangler jeans, a long-sleeved shirt with the tail tucked in, a black felt cowboy hat, boots, and spurs. The spurs Jennie used were not sharp and would not hurt Gypsy. They were simply a way to nudge Gypsy and tell her to speed up.

"Okay, guys," said Jennie. "I'm ready. Let's go to the arena."

Jennie led Gypsy out of the stable and into the arena. The arena was carefully manicured. The dirt needed to be soft enough for Gypsy to get good footing when she ran around the barrels. The dirt had to be disked with a tractor to keep it soft and loose. Jennie preferred riding Gypsy in deep, loose dirt, and she certainly did not want any rocks or hard dirt clods to be in the dirt. They could potentially cause injuries to Gypsy.

Jennie explained to the boys that barrel racing was a timed event. Before she entered the arena, she would get Gypsy up to a running start. They had to ride around each of the three barrels as quickly as they could, and then ride out of the arena at top speed. If a barrel was knocked over, they would receive a five seconds penalty. With that always on her mind, Jennie tried to get close to the barrel, but not so close that either she or Gypsy tipped it over.

The boys found a place along the arena fence to climb upon and sit. Dallas looked around the arena and out into the ranch with all its vast fields of grasslands, barns, cattle, and horses. He loved the beauty of it all, and he liked the smell of the freshly plowed dirt in the arena. In fact, the boys didn't even complain about the smells around the ranch anymore. "Smell that air?" asked Dallas. "I love it!"

"What are you talking about?" asked Justin.

"The ranch has a different smell about it than what we're used to smelling at home," explained Dallas. "It's a mixture of hay, dirt, animals, and clean, fresh air. I could get used to living out here."

"Me, too," said Hank. "I wish we could move out here and live. I'd really like to have a horse of my own and a cow dog. I think I'll be a cowboy when I grow up."

"That does sound like a good idea, Hank, but I don't think Mom and Dad would ever move back here," said Justin. "Dad would have to find a new job. Maybe we could talk to him about it sometime and see what he says."

As they talked, Jennie mounted Gypsy and rode her around the arena several times to help her warm up and stretch her muscles. She started out by walking Gypsy around the arena. Then she picked up the pace by having Gypsy trot a few laps, and then lope around the arena several times. When Jennie felt Gypsy was ready, she rode her to the starting area.

With a burst of speed and energy, Jennie and Gypsy flew into the arena. The boys watched with amazement as Jennie worked with Gypsy to maneuver quickly around each barrel, then pick up speed after the last barrel, and gallop out of the arena.

Jennie and Gypsy trotted up to the boys. "Well, what do you think?" asked Jennie.

"You were great!" said Justin. "Gypsy is a great horse!"

"Do you want to ride her next?" asked Jennie.

Justin looked at Dallas and Hank and then back at Jennie. "Are you sure?" asked Justin.

"Yes, I'm sure," said Jennie. "She's a gentle horse. If you'll get in the saddle, I'll lead her around the arena until you feel comfortable with her."

"Go on, Justin," said Dallas. "I'll take a picture of you with your camera." Dallas had slipped Justin's camera into his pocket when he found out they were going to visit Jennie.

Justin hopped down off the fence, and Jennie helped him get up in the saddle. Justin reached down and stroked Gypsy's mane. He had ridden horses before at the Double A, and he wasn't afraid of riding Gypsy; however, he was a cautious rider because in the past he had witnessed horses getting spooked, rearing up on their back legs, and throwing the rider.

Jennie had the reins in her hand and led Gypsy around the arena. She was a fit and obedient horse. Jennie had trained her well.

Dallas and Hank each had a turn riding Gypsy. They used Justin's camera to get a picture of everyone. Jennie mounted Gypsy one more time for a few more turns around the barrels. After the workout, Jennie removed the tack and hung it up in the horse barn. She asked the boys to help her curry and comb Gypsy before she fed and watered her. Then she turned her loose in the corral.

"Next Saturday, I'm going to race at the rodeo grounds in Granbury. You guys are all invited," said Jennie.

"That sounds like fun!" said an excited Hank. "I'd love to go."

"We'll have to talk to Ace and Ms. Adaline, but I bet we can go," said Justin.

They walked up to the house and heard little J. C. crying, so they knew he was awake. They went into the house to get a drink of water and cool off from the afternoon heat.

"Are we still going to have a barn sale?" asked Jennie.

"I think we should," said Dallas. "Ace helped us get some things out of the barn before Patch had to go to the hospital. I bet we could get some more out before the end of the week."

"I think we should have the sale on Friday." said Jennie. "That would give us time to get it all together. I can come over tomorrow and help get some more stuff out of the barn."

Ms. Adaline knocked on the door. She was there to pick up the boys, but of course, she had to hold J. C. for a few minutes. His big brown eyes were wide open after a good nap. Ms. Adaline enjoyed holding and talking to him as if he understood everything she said. The boys smiled and thought that she probably did the same thing with them when they were babies.

The boys loaded up in Ms. Adaline's Suburban for the ride back to the Double A. Their first week at the ranch had been a busy one, and it looked as if the next one would be, too. They would go see Patch at the hospital in Granbury the next morning, and then they would get busy in the barn sorting the junk. If the barn sale went well, they could go to Fossil Rim.

The boys wished they could stay a little longer at the Double A Ranch. They still had so many things they wanted to do. They especially wanted to hear a few more of Patch's stories before heading back to the "pastures of concrete and asphalt."

CHAPTER 18
FREE AT LAST

PATCH was getting sick and tired of being sick and tired. He was ready to get out of the hospital bed and back to the ranch. He had never spent a week in bed, and he didn't like it one bit. He tried more than once to convince Nurse Lucas that he was supposed to be going home. He even packed up a few of his belongings to head home when she walked in and caught him.

"You get back in that bed, Patch," snapped Nurse Lucas. "What makes you think you are going anywhere?"

"Aw, now, Nurse Lucas, you know good an' well I should be going home," said Patch as he tried to look strong and healthy.

"Patch, take off those boots and get back into bed right now. I have some medication to give you. Your doctor will be here shortly, and he will tell me if it is time for you to go home."

Patch looked down at his boots, sat down on the chair, and pulled them off. He knew he wasn't going anywhere just yet, and he didn't want to cause Nurse Lucas anymore trouble. "Shucks," said Patch. "Just two more minutes, and I'd been out the door and headin' back to the ranch. All right, you win." Patch was disappointed that he wasn't on his way home.

"Here you go, Patch, take this," said Nurse Lucas. "All of it." Patch had a bad habit of taking only part of the medicine and hoping he wouldn't get caught. It never worked.

Patch sat back in bed feeling sorry for himself. All he could do was sit in bed and do nothing. It's hard for a man who has always been a sun-up-to-sun-down working kind of cowboy to sit around and do nothing. This business of getting old and worn out was not going to be easy for Patch. He remembered when he was a teenager and how he didn't want to do anything else except be on his horse taking care of things at his father's ranch. When he went to college, he thought he would take over the ranch once his father retired, but sometimes things don't work out the way you plan them. When he lost his father and grandfather at the same time, he lost the desire to keep on working on the ranch without them. He tried, but everywhere he turned, he saw reminders of the past that haunted him. He made the decision to start fresh somewhere else after college. That was when Rowdy got a job offer at the Double A, and he decided to try to get hired on as a ranch hand, too. Ace was looking for some young cowboys to help him out, and he landed a job right beside Rowdy.

Rowdy was just like a brother to Patch. At one time, they both wanted to ride bulls in the rodeo. They traveled around Texas competing in small town rodeos and paying money to get thrown into the dirt by a thousand pound bull. That was fun for a while, but it didn't pay the bills, and they had to find something that would. That's when they started hiring out at area ranches.

Patch had managed to read a couple of books while he was in the hospital. He reached over to pick up a new book. He hoped the doctor would be there soon to tell him he could go home, and then he'd call Rowdy to come get him.

Patch had just started reading when he heard a light knock on the door, but he couldn't see anyone. "Who's there?" he asked.

"Noah," said someone from behind the door.

Patch looked confused. "Noah? Noah who?"

"Noah cowboy who needs some company?"

Jennie and the boys walked into the room with Ms. Adaline right behind them. Patch was so excited to see them that he jumped up out of bed and gave them all a big hug.

"Now, what are you cowpokes doing here? Ain't you supposed to be mending fences or something?" asked Patch.

"There's plenty of time for that," said Ms. Adaline. "Things were kind of quiet at the ranch, and we thought we'd come by and see if you were behaving yourself."

"Ms. Adaline, I'm so ready to git out of here and git back to work. That doctor of mine is supposed to be here any time now to tell me to put on my boots and go home, but I haven't seen him yet."

Nurse Lucas stuck her head in the room. "Patch, it looks like you have a roomful of visitors! Why don't you take them down to the visitor's waiting room until your doctor gets here? I'll come get you when he gets here."

"That sounds like a good idea. Come on, folks, and I'll show you the way," said Patch.

The boys walked right beside Patch. They looked up at him as they walked down the hall. They thought he looked pretty good for someone who had been in the hospital for a week. Ms. Adaline and Jennie followed along behind the men as they made their way to the waiting room. Once they were seated, Ms. Adaline opened a small paper bag and said, "Here, Patch. This is for you."

She handed him a chocolate milk shake. "Ms. Adaline, you are an angel! I think they've been trying to starve me in this place."

"Now, Patch, Ace told me they were feeding you very well up here," said Ms. Adaline. She gave Patch one of those looks that mothers are good at giving that says, "Don't lie to me, young man."

"Well, I suppose so, but nothin' is as good as that bunkhouse grub Slim fixes up for us," said Patch. He put the straw in his mouth and began sipping on the milk shake. He raised his eyebrows and smacked his lips. Then he rolled it around in his mouth and smacked his lips again. He stopped long enough to smile. "That's mighty fine stuff," he said.

Hank walked over to Patch and said, "We wanted to bring you something." He handed Patch a big sheet of white paper that was folded to look like a card. Patch squinted his eyes and looked at the messages and pictures from all of them.

"Well, now, that's the best card I've ever received in my whole life. Thank you from the bottom of this old heart of mine. I suspect I'll be headed back to the ranch today or tomorrow," said Patch. "When I do, we're gonna have us another campfire talk."

About that time, Nurse Lucas stuck her head in the door of the waiting room. "Patch, your doctor is on his way to your room. You should probably head that way, too."

Patch stood up and said he'd be right back. He walked down the hall toward his room. He tipped his hat at the nurses working at the nurse's station as he passed by them. When he got to his room, his doctor was waiting on him. After a few minutes, Patch returned to the waiting room. "Looks like this ole cowboy's goin' home," said Patch. "I could use some help gittin' my stuff together. Come on down, and give me a hand."

It didn't take long for Patch to get his belongings together and sign the dismissal papers. Ms. Adaline and the kids took his belongings out to the Suburban.

Patch was ready to walk out the door of his room when Nurse Lucas showed up with a wheelchair. "Who needs that thing?" asked Patch.

Nurse Lucas pointed to the wheelchair. "You do. Have a seat."

"I don't need that thing," said Patch.

"Yes, sir, you do. Hospital policy. We push you out in a wheelchair. Now, sit," said Nurse Lucas. She was firm with Patch and didn't want any monkey business from him.

He knew she was not going to change her mind, so he sat down in the wheelchair with a frown on his face. "You can just turn that frown upside down, Patch," said Nurse Lucas. "It's going to be a beautiful day!"

"It's going to be a beautiful day," Patch said in a sing-song voice under his breath. He was more than ready to get back to the bunkhouse.

Ms. Adaline and the kids pulled up in the Suburban in front of the hospital. Nurse Lucas helped Patch get up from the wheelchair. He reached out and gave her a peck on her forehead.

"Thank you, Nurse Lucas. I'm going to miss you bossing me around."

"Oh, get out of here," laughed Nurse Lucas. "It's going to be nice and quiet with you out of here!" She smiled and waved good-bye to Patch and the kids as they drove away from the hospital.

Free at last! Patch could hardly wait to see the Double A again.

CHAPTER 19
Good Catch, Jasper

ROWDY WAS WORKING the cattle in the north pasture when he decided to take a break and get a bottle of cold water from the cooler in the pickup. He took out his kerchief and wiped the sweat off his forehead. He noticed his cell phone in the pickup and checked the messages. There was a message from Ms. Adaline saying she was bringing Patch home from the hospital.

Rowdy hollered out at the ranch hands, "Patch is on his way home. I'll see you guys at the bunkhouse at lunch." Rowdy jumped in the pickup, and Jasper managed to jump in the back before Rowdy took off. He wanted to get to the bunkhouse before Patch did. Rowdy drove as fast as he could without jarring the pickup too much on the bumpy roads in the pasture. He'd forgotten that Jasper was in the pickup bed. Jasper was bouncing back and forth and up and down. Somehow he managed to stay in the pickup, even though all he could hold on with were his toe nails. On the metal floor of the pickup bed, they weren't doing much good.

Rowdy pulled up in front of the bunkhouse, dusted off his jeans, and saw Jasper jump out of the back. Jasper ran up to him with his tail wagging as if he were expecting Rowdy to pat him on the head and tell him what a good job he had done holding on, but Rowdy didn't have time. He jumped up on the porch and flew into the bunkhouse. Slim was standing at the stove stirring a big pot of beans.

"Slim, Patch is on his way home from the hospital and will be here any minute now," said Rowdy with urgency.

"Just relax, Rowdy. I got his bed ready for him this morning. I moved him in the spare room in the back, and he can have it as long as he wants it. Maybe he'll get more rest if he's back there away from the rest of us," said Slim.

"That's great, Slim. Here they come now." Rowdy could see Ms. Adaline turning in at the entrance. Rowdy was as excited as a kid in a candy store knowing that Patch was finally coming home. He stepped out onto the front porch with his hands on his hips and watched them as they drove up to the bunkhouse. Ms. Adaline pulled in the front by the porch steps and stopped. Rowdy went over to the Suburban and opened the door for Patch.

"I dang sure hope you don't have a wheelchair for me," said Patch. "I don't ever want to ride in one of those things again. Just send me my horse, so I know I won't get bucked off." Patch reached out to shake hands with Rowdy. Rowdy took his hand and pulled him closer so that he could give Patch a good bear hug. "Good to see ya, Rowdy," said Patch. "I hope you'll let this ole cowboy git back to work."

"We're ready for you to git back to work, but first things first," said Rowdy. "Let's git you into the bunkhouse." He helped Patch up the steps and then returned to the Suburban to help Ms. Adaline with Patch's belongings.

Once they had everything unloaded, Ms. Adaline said, "I'll see you folks later. I'm going to tell Ace that Patch is home."

"Thank ya kindly, Ms. Adaline, for the ride home," said Patch. "What are you kids gonna do?"

"We are going to go out to the junk barn. We're going to have our barn sale on Friday, and we need to start getting ready," said Jennie. "Come on, guys, let's go!"

Jennie and the boys took off running to the junk barn. On the way, they saw Chester, or rather Chester saw them first. He puffed up big enough to spook anything that came his way and kept a sharp eye on the kids. He wasn't going to let anybody sneak up behind him again. Once the kids were in the barn, Chester went back to hunting and pecking for his snack.

There was a lot of work to get done in the next few days. They moved stuff all afternoon and had quite a large stack of things they wanted Ace to look at to see if they could sell them.

Jasper came running into the barn with his tail wagging. Rowdy had turned him loose on the ranch to run and roam to his heart's content and maybe chase a rabbit or two. He had heard the kids in the barn and decided to see what was going on in there. He made his way to each of the kids so they could pat him on the head, and then he started sniffing around all the junk. When he got tired, he laid down on an old rug by the barn door.

Jasper was curious about what the kids were doing, but between the bouncy ride in the back of Rowdy's pickup and an earlier chase he had with a cottontail rabbit, he had just about run himself ragged. He circled around and flopped down on the old rug. He closed his eyes in hopes of chasing some rabbits in his dreams. It didn't look like Jasper was going to get his wish. A big, black, buzzing horsefly wasn't going to let him get any sleep. A horsefly looks like a regular housefly, but ten times larger. They're big, loud, and pack a big bite.

Jasper twitched his ears every time the horsefly buzzed around his head. He hoped that some kind of movement would scare it off, but evidently Jasper had forgotten how sticky horseflies can be. You can shoo them away, but they never go very far, and they return so quickly you never have a chance to miss them. Jasper twitched his ears several times, and then he started snapping at it. He opened his eyes while his head was still down on his paws pretending he wasn't paying attention to the fly. When the fly buzzed around his head, he jerked his head up quickly and snapped at it.

Jasper tried his best to get rid of the horsefly, but all he could do was snap at the air. It was as if Jasper could hear that fly making fun of him, and it just kept on taunting him. Every time he buzzed around Jasper, he got more and more aggravated.

Hank noticed Jasper snapping at the fly first. "Hey, Justin, watch Jasper."

Justin giggled. "What's he going to do with that thing if he catches it?"

About that time, Jasper managed to snap at the horsefly and catch it. Startled, he jumped up on all four legs and shook his head with his tongue hanging out trying to get the fly off the end of his tongue. Hank and Justin laughed at poor Jasper. They went over and patted him on the head. "Good catch, Jasper," laughed Hank. "Now maybe you can get a nap."

Hank and Justin got back to work. Dallas was in the back of the barn looking through some old camping equipment. "Hey, guys, I found a tent," he said. "Can somebody come help me with it?"

Jennie was close by. "Here, I'll help you, Dallas," she said. She climbed over a couple of boxes and got to where Dallas was looking. The tent was in a canvas bag that closed with a zipper. Jennie got one end of it, Dallas got the other, and they started out of the barn.

They dropped it on the ground, and dust flew everywhere. Jasper jumped up on all fours again. He gave up on taking a nap and went over to check out what Jennie and Dallas were doing. They took out all the poles and stakes and placed them on the ground. Then, they took out the tent.

"That's cool," said Hank. "Let's go camping!"

"Yeah, let's go camping," said Dallas. "Ms. Adaline has some sleeping bags in the closet in the den."

"We can't go camping until we finish getting ready for the barn sale," said Justin. "Why don't we just leave the tent here and ask Ace and Ms. Adaline later if we can camp out one night while we're here?"

"That sounds good to me," said Dallas.

About mid-afternoon, the kids headed up to the Main House. Jasper walked along behind them but took off in a trot toward the bunkhouse when he got close to it. He could hear Rowdy and Patch talking as they sat on the front porch drinking a jar of sweet tea.

Jennie and the boys had forgotten about stopping for lunch and were hungry. They opened the front door and stepped inside. They headed straight toward the kitchen to see if Ms. Adaline had something they could eat. "Ms. Adaline, we found…" said Dallas.

Ms. Adaline stopped him before he could finish. "All of you go back outside and dust yourselves off. Then go straight to the wash room, and wash your hands with soap, then we'll talk."

When they finished, Ms. Adaline asked, "What are you kiddos hungry for?"

"Anything, Ms. Adaline. I'm so hungry I could eat an elephant!" said Jennie.

"Why don't I fix you some peanut butter and jelly sandwiches and a big glass of cold milk?"

"Perfect!" said Jennie, and the boys agreed.

"Dallas, what did you find in the junk barn?" asked Ms. Adaline as she put out eight slices of bread on the countertop.

"We found a tent in a bag. Could we camp out one night while we're here?" asked Dallas.

"Sure, you can. But you're going to have to figure out how to set it up. I can't help you with that, I'm afraid."

They all smiled at each other pleased they could look forward to an adventure under the moon and stars, but they knew they would have to have some help. Justin was thinking that maybe Rowdy could help them. He took a big bite of his sandwich and thought he would ask Rowdy after supper when they were at the campfire. Justin hoped Patch would join them tonight and tell them another story. He had missed Patch much more than he had realized.

CHAPTER 20

Lizzie Johnson, Cattle Baroness

AFTER JENNIE AND THE BOYS ate supper with Ace and Ms. Adaline, the kids went outside. The sun was still up, and the heat from the day hung heavily in the air. It would cool off after the sun went down, but for the moment it was still above 90 degrees. They sat down on the front porch of the Main House to wait until they saw the ranch hands start up the campfire.

"How long are you going to be here tonight, Jennie?" asked Justin.

"Dad said I could stay until after the campfire time. I'm supposed to call him when we get through," she said. "He told me he was working on the flyers for the barn sale and would bring them with him whenever he came to pick me up."

"Jennie, aren't you supposed to have a barrel racing competition on Saturday?" asked Dallas.

"Yes, I was hoping y'all could come out and watch," said Jennie.

"Isn't that the day we were going to try to go Fossil Rim?" asked Dallas.

"Oh, yeah," said Jennie. "There's no way we could do both of those things on the same day. What are we going to do?"

"Let's go ahead and have the barn sale on Friday," said Justin. "Maybe we can stay a day or two longer and go to Fossil Rim on one of those days."

"Guys, I've been thinking about what we could do with the money we make from the barn sale," said Dallas. "You know, we could do something else with it."

"So, what are you thinking about?" asked Hank.

"This is just a thought, but maybe we can do something nice for someone in the hospital," said Dallas.

"I'm sure there is," said Justin, "but I don't know what it would be. We could ask Ms. Adaline or Patch or Rowdy. They might have a suggestion."

"Great idea," said Jennie. "I'd like to do something to help someone who really needs it. Dallas, that is a very thoughtful suggestion."

"Thanks, Jennie," said Dallas as he looked down somewhat embarrassed.

As the summer sun began to set in the western sky, the cowboys began to come out of the bunkhouse a few at a time and mill around the yard. Several of them headed toward the campfire. Rowdy and Patch were already standing by the fire, and the kids decided to join them.

As they approached the campfire, Jasper came running up to them. His tail was wagging so hard he could hardly stand up. Justin reached out and gave him a good rub down. "Hi, Jasper," said Justin. "Let's go see what's happening around the campfire."

Jennie and the boys went over and gave Patch and Rowdy a hug before they sat down by the smoky fire. They noticed that Slim had brought out some wire coat hangers and marshmallows so the kids could toast them over the fire.

"Grab yourselves a coat hanger and a handful of marshmellers," said Slim. "We're gonna toast us up some goodies tonight to celebrate Patch's homecoming!"

The kids grinned as they put the marshmallows on the wire hangers. "I like mine burned just a little," said Jennie.

"Me, too!" said Hank. He stood right beside Jennie so he could watch how she turned her marshmallow over and over in the fire. Every now and then, it would get a small flame on it, and she would blow it out.

"Did cowboys used to toast marshmallows out on the cattle trail?" asked Dallas.

"Naw," said Slim. "I don't think those cowboys even knew about marshmellers, and I just can't see them danglin' marshmellers over the campfire."

"Were there any women cattle drivers out on the cattle trails?" asked Jennie.

"Yes, but they were few and far between," said Patch, "but let me tell you one thing, Ms. Jennie. The men of early Texas couldn't have done what they did without the women helpin' 'em out. The women did all kinds of work in early Texas, and some of it was the same kind of work that still has to be done today. They did the cookin', cleanin', and raisin' the children, and sometimes they had to do a lot more than that. If their husband got killed or sick or hurt, they had to do all the ranchin' as well."

"It sounds as if women were expected to do a lot of really hard work back then," said Jennie.

"Yes, ma'am, they certainly were," said Patch. "When the kids got old enough to help out, they were expected to work on the ranch just like Rowdy and me did. We started workin' on our ranches when we were no bigger than a June bug."

"Today in the junk barn I found this old picture," said Jennie. She reached into her pocket and pulled out an old photo that was printed on the back of a post card. She handed the picture to Patch.

"That's Lizzie Johnson," said Patch. "Now this young lady was a cattle baron, or I guess I should say *baroness*."

Patch turned to Hank and said, "Cowboy, would you go git me one of them marshmellers from Slim? I'm thinkin' I could use a toasted treat."

"Yes, sir!" said Hank. He jumped up and went over to Slim. The big bag of marshmallows was almost empty, but Slim handed him two so that he could toast two at a time. Hank put the marshmallows over the fire and kept a sharp eye on them. When they were nice and toasty, he held the coat hanger close to Patch so he could pull the first one off by himself.

"Here you go, Patch," said Hank.

Patch pulled it off the wire, popped it into his mouth, and smacked his lips. The sticky marshmallow stuck to his beard just around his mouth. Every time he tried to clean it off, he smeared it a little bit more. He tried to wipe it off by rubbing his mouth along his shirt sleeve, but that didn't help. Finally, he gave up and said, "Well, Dadgumit. I've got this sticky stuff everywhere."

Dallas jumped up and said, "Hold on, Patch. I'll be right back." He ran into the bunkhouse and came out with a wet paper towel. As he stepped off the porch, he spotted something dart in front of him and run under the porch. Dallas hollered, "Rowdy, come quick!"

Rowdy jumped up from the campfire and took off running to see what was wrong. He thought Dallas was hurt. "What's the matter?"

"Something just ran in front of me and under the porch," said Dallas.

"I can tell you right now what it was," said Rowdy. "Can't you smell it?"

Rowdy got down on his right knee and looked under the bunkhouse. He could see the beady eyes of a skunk looking back at him. The last thing Rowdy wanted was for that skunk to spray.

Rowdy looked at Dallas and said, "You come on down, and git back to the fire. I've got to try to git that skunk out from under there."

Dallas took off running toward the fire. "Here's a wet paper towel for your face, Patch," said Dallas. "Rowdy's going to get a skunk out from under the bunkhouse."

"Is that what you were yellin' about over there?" asked Patch as he wiped his lips and beard with the wet paper towel.

"All right, now," said Patch. "Let me tell you about Ms. Lizzie Johnson while Rowdy tries to run that skunk out. If you see that skunk running this way, git up quick and head for the Main House."

Patch refocused and began, "Now, Lizzie Johnson was one of those women who came to Texas as a little girl and decided to git out from under the shade tree and make a difference. She went to school and became a teacher, but then she started helping cattlemen keep business records for their ranches. She started learning about the cattle business and decided she wanted some cattle of her own. She also liked to write stories, and she sold some to a magazine in New York City. She wrote her stories using a 'pen name.' That means she used somebody else's name as the author. Back then, they sometimes didn't print much of anything written by a woman, so she used a man's name. It was all a big secret. No one knows for sure what she wrote or what name she used. When she got paid for those stories, she spent that money to buy some cattle for herself.

"She also bought some land and was the boss of her cattle business. When it came time to send the cattle to market, she herded those cattle clean across the state of Texas by herself. Can you imagine that? She worked as hard as any man did on a ranch."

"Did she have a family?" asked Jennie.

"Well, she finally got married when she was about thirty-nine, but she had her husband sign a pre-nuptial agreement. That means her husband agreed that Ms. Lizzie's money and property belonged only to her. She ended up with a lot of money, bought all kinds of fancy stuff, and took expensive trips.

"When Ms. Lizzie and her husband were visiting in Cuba, he got himself kidnapped. Ms. Lizzie had to pay some money to git him back. He died several years after that, and Ms. Lizzie wasn't ever quite the same. She stayed at home all the time and hid her money in the house. When she died in 1924, her family cleaned out her house and found money poked in holes all over that house. She was a wealthy woman, but she didn't have a penny in the bank except the Bank of Ms. Lizzie Johnson, that is."

About that time, Slim saw something running out from under the bunkhouse porch. He stood up, pointed toward the bunkhouse, and yelled, "Run! Here comes that skunk!"

Sure enough, Rowdy had chased the skunk out from under the bunkhouse, and it was headed straight toward the campfire. Everyone took off in all directions, and the kids headed down the road to the Main House. Ace and Ms. Adaline stepped out onto the porch to see what all the commotion was about.

"I smell a skunk!" said Ms. Adaline. "You kids better get in here before it gets you." Before they could get inside the house, they turned around and saw Patch high-stepping it onto the porch. "Come on, Patch," said Ms. Adaline. We've got room for you, too."

They could hear Rowdy yelling at his cow dog, "Jasper, run *away* from the skunk, not towards it! I don't want you to catch that skunk!" It was too late. The skunk had given Jasper his best shot. They could see Jasper running to the bunkhouse with his tail tucked between his legs.

"Aw, Jasper," said Rowdy. "When are you going to learn not to mess with a skunk?" Then they could hear Rowdy shout, "Slim, do you have any tomato juice to wash this skunk dog with?"

Poor Jasper. He would have to endure a bath in tomato juice and sleep out on the bunkhouse porch. His day would have been perfect had it not been for a pesky horsefly and a smelly skunk. Oh, the joys of being a cow dog on the Double A Ranch!

CHAPTER 21
BARN SALE

THE DAY OF THE BARN SALE finally arrived. Jennie and her dad, Mr. Dilka, arrived at the Double A Ranch bright and early. They put up signs and balloons around the entrance. Although Mr. Dilka was on his way to work, he promised to help Jennie get things ready for the sale. After tying the balloons to the entrance gate, he gave Jennie a quick hug and a kiss and wished her luck. Ace and Ms. Adaline stepped out of the house and gave him a big wave to let him know they would take care of Jennie.

Ace got the boys up early, and Ms. Adaline fixed breakfast for all of them. Ace and Rowdy's responsibilities were to take their pickups down to the junk barn, load up as much stuff as they could, and haul it down to the entrance gate. The barn sale items would be set just inside the front gate. Ms. Adaline's job was to set up the money table and set out the items after Ace and Rowdy unloaded them from the pickup. Jennie and the boys would help wherever they were needed.

It wasn't long before people started arriving. Car after car and pickup after pickup arrived at the Double A Ranch loaded with men, women, and children of all ages. They bought big items and small items. Hank brought his wagon loaded with rocks collected from the ranch. He had washed them, cleaned them, and put a sign on the wagon that said, "Rocks for Sale - 25¢ each."

About noon, Slim hooked up some horses to the chuck wagon and hauled it down to the entrance. He opened it up and set out some bowls and spoons. He started a fire to heat up a big pot of chili made at the bunkhouse. He set out a big pan of cornbread and a container of sweet tea and shouted, "Come and git it!"

"Boy, I'm hungry," said Justin. "This looks good!" Justin loaded up a bowl of chili, got a big piece of cornbread and headed toward an empty chair. He took a big bite of chili and said, "This is good stuff! Dallas, would you please bring me some tea?"

Dallas brought some tea over to Justin, and then he spotted Patch coming out of the bunkhouse and said, "Here comes Patch. I think I'll go out and meet him."

Dallas took off running toward Patch. When he was within talking distance of him, Dallas said, "Hi, Patch! How are you feeling?"

"Howdy, partner! I'm feeling just peachy! I thought I'd better come down and see what was going on."

"We've sold a lot of stuff. Hank has even sold some rocks!" laughed Dallas.

"You mean he's trying to sell some of those rocks just like his daddy did? Craziest thing I've ever heard of," said Patch. He shook his head as he thought about what some people will buy. "It looks like you're gonna need the sheriff's posse to help you git all that money to the bank. What are you gonna do with all that money anyway?"

"That's a good question," said Dallas. "We wanted to go to Fossil Rim over in Glen Rose, but we're not going to have time to go before my mom and dad come to pick us up. We started thinking that we could use the money to do something nice for someone, but we don't know who or how. Do you have any suggestions?"

"Now, that's a mighty nice thought, cowboy," said Patch. "We should always be lookin' for ways to help our friends and neighbors. But, don't forgit we've got some four-legged friends who could use some help, too. There's an animal shelter in Acton that takes in animals who need a home. They are always in need of help with food and such. You might want to keep them in mind."

"Thanks, Patch," said Dallas. "I'll talk to the others about it later."

As they approached the chuck wagon, Slim said, "Here ya go, Patch." He handed Patch a bowl of hot chili.

"Thanks, Slim. I heard you had hauled this chuck wagon down here for lunch. If you'll ring that triangle on the corner of the wagon, the rest of those hungry cowboys will head out this way. They sent me out here to scout out the food," said Patch. "They were wonderin' where you had run off to."

"Dallas, why don't you try your hand at ringin' that dinner triangle?" asked Slim. Dallas reached up and grabbed the metal stick hanging on a string next to the triangle. He made a circle inside the triangle and hit all three sides. It didn't take long for the hands to walk outside and start toward the entrance to the ranch. Within a few minutes, they were lined up at the chuck wagon ready to chow down.

Hank pulled his red wagon down the line as the cowboys waited their turn to eat. "Rocks for sale! Twenty-five cents! Who wants a nice, clean rock?"

"Gimme one of those, cowboy," said a skinny cowboy named Shorty. "Come on, you guys. You need to buy yourself one of these fine rocks!" They each reached into their pockets and gave Hank a quarter. By the time he got to the end of the line, all of the rocks were gone.

Patch watched as they picked out rocks one-by-one. He shook his head as he tried to figure out what they were going to do with them. "Craziest thing I ever heard of," he said under his breath.

About three o'clock, Ms. Adaline said, "Let's pick up all of this stuff we didn't sell, and put it in those boxes over there. I don't think anybody else is going to buy any more of our junk today. Rowdy will come pick it all up later and take it to Goodwill."

Jennie and the boys packed up the boxes and had everything in one place ready for Rowdy to pick up. They each picked up a chair or card table and walked up to the Main House. They were exhausted from the work and the heat. Ms. Adaline fixed a big pitcher of ice-cold lemonade, and they sat at the kitchen table to enjoy it.

"I'm proud of the way you kids worked today," said Ms. Adaline. "It was a lot of fun to see some of my friends and neighbors sorting through that junk and finding things they could use. Right now, I'm going to move over to the breakfast bar and count the money. While I'm doing that, y'all need to decide what you're going to do with it."

Jennie and the boys were so tired all they could do was sit and look at each other. After they took a few sips of their lemonade,

Dallas spoke up. "I talked to Patch a little bit this afternoon to see if he could give us any ideas on how we could help someone with our money. I thought he had a pretty good suggestion. He said there is an animal shelter in Acton that takes in animals that are not wanted by their owners anymore. The people at the shelter give them a place to live until they can be adopted by a new owner. All of that food and care takes money. Patch suggested we buy some dog and cat food and donate it to the shelter. If we had money left over, we could just donate it to the shelter to cover some of their other expenses. What do y'all think?"

"My friend has a dog that she got from that shelter," said Jennie. "It's a great dog, and it was so happy to be rescued. I think that is a great idea!" Justin and Hank agreed.

"I don't know about you guys," said Justin, "but I can hardly wait to see how much money we made."

Ms. Adaline smiled. "You should be proud of yourselves! You made $643.25!"

"Wow!" said Jennie. "That's a lot of money!"

Dallas, Justin, and Hank stood up and did a victory dance. Jennie laughed at how silly they looked. For some reason, they didn't feel so tired anymore. "Let's go buy some dog food!" said Justin.

Ms. Adaline stood up from the breakfast bar and said, "We'll do that later. Right now, this old lady wants to rest her weary bones before she fixes some supper. We can buy dog food tomorrow." Ms. Adaline washed her hands and headed for the bedroom for a nap. She had worked hard at the barn sale, and she certainly deserved some time to rest.

CHAPTER 22
MISS KITTY

SATURDAY WAS SHAPING into a busy day. Jennie had her barrel racing event in Granbury, and the boys wanted to buy dog and cat food for the animal shelter. The boys also knew their mom and dad would be coming to pick them up. They weren't ready to go home. There were still many things they were hoping to do while visiting on the Double A. They wanted to camp out in the tent they found in the junk barn and hear more campfire stories. They also wanted to visit Elizabeth Crockett's statue.

Rowdy and Patch took the boys to buy large bags of dog and cat food from a local feed and ranch store. They spent about $300 on food, and the remainder of the money for the animal shelter was put in an envelope.

They pulled up in front of an old house that had been remodeled into an animal shelter. The boys jumped out of Rowdy's pickup and went inside. They were greeted by a very nice lady named

Dixie dressed in jeans and a Granbury High School t-shirt. Her short hair was dark, and her blue eyes sparkled when she smiled at the boys.

After introducing themselves to Dixie, Dallas said, "We'd like to give you some food for the dogs and cats."

"How wonderful!" said Dixie. "We seem to go through food so quickly around here. You can put it over here." She pointed to a small shelf.

"I don't think we can put the food we brought on that shelf," said Hank. "We've got some really large bags."

"Maybe I should go see for myself what you have so I can find a good place for it," said Dixie. She and the boys walked outside where Rowdy and Patch were standing beside the pickup.

"Howdy, ma'am," said Rowdy and Patch as they greet Dixie and tipped their hats in a gentlemanly gesture.

"Where would you like for us to put these bags of food?" asked Rowdy.

"Oh, my goodness," said Dixie. "I never dreamed you boys brought us dog and cat food in fifty pound bags! This is just wonderful!" She led them to a storage area beside the shelter and asked them to put the bags in there.

When they had done that, Justin said, "We also have some money to donate to the shelter. We had a barn sale yesterday at the Double A Ranch, and we decided to give what we made to the animal shelter. We hope you will be able to use it to pay some veterinarian bills or use on something you need for the shelter."

Dixie's blue eyes watered up a bit from gratitude. She was touched that some children would work hard at a barn sale in order to help the animal shelter. She looked in the envelope that had the remainder of the barn sale money in it.

"There's about $340.00 in there," said Hank. "I even sold some rocks for twenty-five cents each! We hope you will be able to help lots of animals with that money."

"Oh, my goodness, boys," said Dixie. "We can do a lot with this money. Thank you so much. You will never know how much I appreciate this. While you are here, would you like to look around at our dogs and cats?"

The boys looked at Rowdy to see if it would be okay. He nodded his head. "Don't be long, boys," he said. "We still have things to do today."

Dixie led the boys on a quick tour of the shelter. They saw lots of dogs and cats in all sizes, shapes, colors, and breeds. A small black kitten followed them around as they looked at the animals. Dallas noticed the kitten first. He nudged Justin and pointed to it. Justin knew it wouldn't be long before Dallas picked it up. When he couldn't stand it any longer, Dallas reached down and picked up the kitten. She started purring when Dallas rubbed his hand over her silky black coat.

"That's Miss Kitty," said Dixie. "She came here a couple of days ago along with her brothers and sisters. They were all adopted yesterday except for Miss Kitty. She is the last one from the litter still here. Do you know of anyone who needs a pet or a barn cat?"

"No, ma'am, I don't," said Dallas, "but she sure is cute." Dallas put her back down on the floor and started toward the door with Justin and Hank. Miss Kitty ran after Dallas purring and uttering a soft meow that sounded sad. Dallas kept walking away, but Miss

Kitty didn't want him to leave her. At last, he bent down and picked her up again.

"Rowdy, can I keep this kitten?" asked Dallas. "I bet she'll be a good barn cat for the junk barn. Please, Rowdy."

Justin and Hank joined in on the begging. "Please, Rowdy, please."

Patch looked at Rowdy, shook his head, and said, "I'll tell you what I'll do. I'll take the cat, but you boys will have to take care of her whenever you're at the ranch."

"Yea, Patch! You're our hero!" said Dallas. He ran over to Patch and gave him a big hug. All the boys grinned from ear to ear. Justin kept an eye on Patch, and he could see a faint smile under his wiry beard.

After all the paperwork was complete, Rowdy, Patch, the boys, and Miss Kitty loaded up in Rowdy's pickup one more time. They waved good-bye to Dixie and headed back to the ranch. The boys felt good about helping the animal shelter and finding a good home for Miss Kitty. She would make a fine addition to the Double A.

"Now, let's just hope Ace will be as happy about a new barn cat as we are," said Justin.

CHAPTER 23

Barrel Racing at the Rodeo

MISS KITTY was introduced to the junk barn when the boys returned to the Double A Ranch. Food and water were placed in a spot close to the doors. The boys made a bed for her with the rug that Jasper had tried to take a nap on earlier. Miss Kitty seemed happy and perfectly at ease in her new home. There was plenty for her to explore in the barn and keep her entertained. The boys were ready to go to the rodeo grounds with Ace and Ms. Adaline. They were anxious to watch Jennie and Gypsy in the barrel racing event.

Jennie arrived at the rodeo grounds about mid-morning. Gypsy was brought out of the horse trailer and tied to a post near the riding arena. Jennie had fed and watered Gypsy earlier that morning. She was ready to ride, but Jennie wanted her to get used to the sights and sounds of the arena before the competition. Gypsy needed to be comfortable with her surroundings in order to perform well.

Jennie was one of the youngest riders there. She knew there was a lot for her to learn from the other girls who were racing, and she was keenly aware of what they were doing prior to the race. Some of the girls had their dads or brothers taking care of their horses, but Jennie wanted to do it herself. She stayed close to Gypsy, and talked to her to help her stay calm. She put a string of large beads around Gypsy's neck for good luck. Then, Jennie walked her around the rodeo grounds.

About an hour before the barrel racing event began, Jennie mounted Gypsy and began trotting her around the arena to warm-up and stretch her muscles. Once that was done, Jennie kicked her into a full run across the arena. Gypsy was ready for her turn around the barrels.

The cheering section from the Double A joined the other citizens of Hood County in the stands. The outdoor rodeo grounds were typical of those in other small towns in Texas. The stands surrounded a large dirt arena. Chutes and holding pens for the bulls and horses were at one end. There was also a large entry for other events like barrel racing. The arena had lights located on tall poles around the arena for evening events. The stands were full of families representing many generations. Spectators of all ages were dressed in boots, hats, jeans, and western shirts.

The announcer began by welcoming the people in the stands and asking the crowd to stand for the presentation of the flags. Two horse riders entered the arena at the same time. One rider carried the American flag, and the other carried the Texas flag while patriotic music played from the loud speakers. As the flags entered the arena, cowboys and cowgirls respectfully removed their hats and held them over their hearts. The cowboys picked up their speed with each completed ride around the arena as the music continued to play. By the time the music was almost over, the horses were galloping around the arena at full speed. The flags were flying in the wind from the speed of the riders, and the crowd was cheering loudly.

At the end of the song, the horses walked to the center of the arena and stopped. The announcer asked the crowd to remain standing for a prayer, pledge to the American flag, and the National Anthem. This was followed by the pledge to the Texas flag and the state song, "Texas, Our Texas." The boys had learned the song in music class at school and sang all the words with confidence. "Texas, Our Texas, all hail the mighty state. Texas, Our Texas, so wonderful, so great." As the song ended, the crowd cheered again.

Then the announcer said, "Ladies and gentlemen, our nation was created by people who were inspired to live in a nation of freedom. Today, we celebrate the goodness of America by remembering our founding fathers, the defenders of freedom who over the years have been willing to take up arms and fight on our behalf, and the men and women who are still defending us today. Yes, ladies and gentlemen, we are proud to be Americans right here in Hood County, Texas. If you are a veteran of the U. S. Army, Navy, Marines, Air Force, or Coast Guard, please wave, and let us show you how much we appreciate your service on behalf of our nation." Men and women waved all over the arena, and as they did, the crowd cheered loudly.

The announcer continued, "Ladies and gentlemen, you may be seated. It is time for us to begin the barrel racing event." As he finished his sentence, a Border collie just like Jasper, ran into and around the arena at full speed with a monkey in a small saddle strapped on his back. The monkey was dressed as a cowboy complete with a cowboy hat. "Now, wait a minute here, folks. It looks like we have a special guest. Say hello to the best cowboy monkey in these parts, Bucky and his sheep herding dog, Radar." At that moment, a small herd of sheep were sent into the arena. Radar was trained to round-up sheep on a ranch. He zipped and darted all over the arena chasing the sheep and maneuvering them into a marked off area. Every time he zipped and darted, Bucky, who was securely fastened to him, would jerk around in all directions. He would almost fall off one side and then the other. Then he would try to catch his breath as Radar crouched on the ground eyeing the sheep. Without moving a muscle, Radar watched the sheep intently. Bucky used these calm moments to look around at the crowd and adjust his little cowboy hat tied on his head. Just when he wasn't expecting it, Radar would take off again at full speed. Bucky would lean back in his saddle and almost fall off. The crowd roared with laughter. Justin, Dallas, and Hank laughed harder than anyone around them. They had never seen anything so funny in all their lives!

At last, the sheep were all standing in the marked off area, and the announcer said, "Good job, Bucky and Radar! Let's give them a big hand, folks!" Then Radar managed to herd the sheep out of the arena as the crowd continued to cheer them on.

"Now, ladies and gentlemen, let's give a big Hood County welcome to our barrel racing contestants!" The boys could hardly wait to see Jennie compete in her first barrel racing event. They kept their fingers crossed that she would do well. After several other riders, it was Jennie's turn.

The announcer said, "Now, folks, let's give a big welcome to Jennie Dilka, our youngest contestant here today!" Jennie and Gypsy came flying out into the arena. Gypsy was fast and maneuvered around the barrels without knocking over any of them. After the last barrel, Jennie gave Gypsy a few over and under slaps with a strap tied to the saddle horn to encourage her to pick up speed on the way home to the finish line. The boys jumped up and down and cheered for Jennie. Hank took off his cowboy hat and waved it around his head in all the excitement. Jennie had a great race, and they were proud of her.

After a few more riders, the barrel racing event was over, and Jennie won third place. Jennie's parents and J. C. joined Ace and Ms. Adaline in the stands. Mr. Dilka said, "Thanks for coming out and supporting Jennie. She was hoping you would make it."

"We've been looking forward to this all week," said Ms. Adaline. "We wouldn't have missed this for anything."

"She did great!" said Justin.

"She's worked hard over the past weeks to train Gypsy. We're proud of her," said Mrs. Dilka.

"We're going to help her with Gypsy right now, and then we'll be back in the stands to watch the rest of the rodeo," said Mr. Dilka. "Boys, I know you'll be going back to the city in the next day or two. We've enjoyed having you around this summer. I know Jennie has enjoyed combing through the junk barn and hearing some of the campfire stories. I hope you will come back soon."

"Thank you, Mr. Dilka," said Justin. "We enjoyed it, too."

Ace and Ms. Adaline decided they needed to get back to the Double A. It was late in the afternoon, and they were expecting the boys' parents to come in. The boys needed to say good-bye to Rowdy, Patch, Slim, and the other ranch hands before they left. They also needed to break the news to Ace about Miss Kitty.

On the way home, Dallas asked Ace, "Don't you think you need a barn cat to keep the mice and rats out of the junk barn?"

"I've never really thought about it, Dallas," said Ace. "Do you think I might need one?"

"Yes, sir, I do," said Dallas.

"We saw some kittens at the animal shelter today, Ace," said Hank.

"You did?" asked Ace. "Did you see any black ones?"

"Yes, sir, we did," said Hank.

"Ace, what would you think if we brought home a kitten for the barn?" asked Justin.

"You mean like that black one I saw at the junk barn?" asked Ace. He had known all along they had brought Miss Kitty back from the animal shelter. He was just waiting to see how long it would take them to finally tell him.

"You already knew?" asked a surprised Dallas.

"I can always use a good barn cat," said Ace. "Let's hope she can catch a few snakes, too. She needs to earn her keep on the ranch."

The boys smiled at each other. What they thought was going to be a difficult situation, turned out to be an easy one.

When Ace pulled up in front of the Main House at the Double A, the boys took off running to the junk barn to check on Miss Kitty. It looked like she had Ace's seal of approval and would be staying.

CHAPTER 24
THE LAST CAMPFIRE

JUSTIN, DALLAS, AND HANK were in the junk barn when they heard a vehicle honking at the Main House. They knew that would be their parents who were coming to take them home. Their emotions were mixed. They were anxious to see their parents and tell them all they had been doing on the ranch, but they were disappointed that they would be leaving the Double A.

"Come on, guys," said Justin. "We need to go see Mom and Dad." They took off running toward the Main House. When they ran by the chickens, Chester stopped to stare at the boys. He puffed up long enough to send them a reminder of who was in charge around the hen house.

The boys bounded up the front steps of the Main House and flew into the living room. Their parents were talking with Ace and Ms. Adaline and drinking some iced tea.

"Well, looky here," said Ace. "Boys, are you ready to go home?"

"No!" they all said in unison.

"What?" asked their dad. "You mean I drove all the way out here for nothing? I suppose I could turn around and go home and leave you boys here."

"Aw, Dad," said Hank. "We're just teasing. We've had a really good time since we've been here."

After the boys had given each of their parents a hug, they went into the kitchen. Ms. Adaline had prepared a big meal for everyone to enjoy. It seemed as though everyone had something to talk about, and the conversation never ended. The boys talked about the campfire stories they had heard, the junk barn, the barn sale, Jennie and Gypsy, Patch going to the hospital, Miss Kitty, Chester chasing them, and on and on. They had certainly had a fun and busy two weeks on the Double A Ranch.

The boys' dad told them they would not be heading back into the city until the next morning. That meant the boys had one more night at the campfire with the cowboys. After the meal was over, they helped to clear the table.

"You boys can go do whatever you want to do," said Ms. Adaline. "Your mom and I will take care of the dishes while you go play."

"Thank you, Ms. Adaline," said Dallas. "I was hoping we could go to the campfire tonight."

"Sure you can!" said Ms. Adaline. "Now, scoot!"

"Watch out for skunks!" warned Ace. He laughed and began telling the boys' parents about the episode with Jasper and the skunk.

The boys grabbed their cowboy hats and headed out the door to see if the campfire was going yet. They could see Rowdy headed out that way, and so they took off running.

"Rowdy, Ace said we could keep Miss Kitty!" shouted Dallas.

"That's good," said Rowdy. "She and Jasper have already become friends." He pointed toward the bunkhouse. Jasper was sleeping on the front porch with Miss Kitty snuggled up right beside him sound asleep. The boys laughed at the sight of it. It looked as if things were going to work out just fine for Miss Kitty. They were glad they had rescued her from the animal shelter.

Patch walked out of the bunkhouse with a small box in his hands. As he approached the campfire, he said, "Howdy, boys. I thought you might be headed into the city tonight."

"No, sir," said Justin. "not tonight. Dad said we'd leave in the morning."

"That's good," said Patch. "I've got a game for us to play tonight."

"Cool!" said Hank. "I like playing games."

"Well, this game is gonna teach you a thing or two about Texas," said Patch. "You ready to get started?"

"Sure!" said Hank.

Several of the other cowboys joined them at the campfire. When everyone was seated, Patch opened the box.

"We're gonna play 'Texas Trivia,' or at least my version of it," said Patch. "I'll ask the questions, and you fire back the answers. Keep score if you want to, but that's not what's important." Patch scratched his chin through his beard and said, "Are you ready?"

"We're ready," said Rowdy. "Let's see what kind of trivia you have for us."

"We'll go around the circle so be ready when it's your turn. Rowdy, you go first. Hank, you're the cow's tail," said Patch.

"Cow's tail?" asked Hank.

"That means you're last, cowboy," said Patch. "Here's the first question. What city is the state capital of Texas?"

"Austin," said Rowdy.

"Right," said Patch. "Justin, what is the state flower of Texas?"

"Blucbonnct."

"Right," said Patch. "Dallas, what is the state tree of Texas?"

"Pecan, just like that one," said Dallas as he pointed to the pecan tree in front of the Main House.

"Right," said Patch. "Hank, what is the state bird of Texas?"

"Mockingbird," said Hank. "Justin, do you remember when that mockingbird pecked you on the head?" Hank laughed.

"Yes, I remember," said Justin. "It scared me to death!"

"Mockingbird is correct, Hank," said Patch. "Rowdy, it's your turn again. How many counties are there in Texas?"

"Well, let me think," said Rowdy. "I think there are 254 counties. Is that right?"

"Yep, that's right," said Patch. "You cowboys are doing pretty well at this game. Justin, can you tell me the name of the first President of the Republic of Texas?"

"That's easy," said Justin. "It was Sam Houston!"

"You're right," said Patch. "Dallas, who is known as the Father of Texas?"

"I know this one," said Dallas. "It was Stephen F. Austin, and Sam Houston is the one who gave that title to him."

"Yep," said Patch. "Hank, what is the name of the State Song of Texas?"

"That's easy. We sang it today at the rodeo. It's 'Texas, Our Texas.'"

"Good, Hank," said Patch. "Okay, now cowboys, the questions are going to get harder. Rowdy, it's your turn. What is the official state mascot?"

"Well, it had better not be a skunk!" laughed Rowdy. "Let me see. It could be a prairie dog or a possum or an armadillo. I think I'll say it's the armadillo."

"Good guess, Rowdy," said Patch. "It's the armadillo, all right. Now, Justin, what is the official state motto?"

"The official state motto of Texas," said Justin, "is Friendship."

"Right!" said Patch. "I thought I would get you on that one! Okay, Dallas, it's your turn. If I wanted to visit the place where the Texas Declaration of Independence was written and signed, where would I go?"

"I know that one because we went there on a field trip," said Dallas. "Washington-on-the-Brazos."

"Right," said Patch. "Hank, how many stars are on the Texas flag?"

"Let me see, now," said Hank. He rested his finger on the side of his chin and tapped it as if he were thinking, but really he was just stalling. He knew the answer to this question. "One," he said at last. "That's why Texas is called the Lone Star State."

"Right," said Patch. "Rowdy, this is the last round of questions. What is the state gem of Texas?"

"State gym?" asked Rowdy. "You mean a gym where you play basketball?"

"Not a gym. Clean out your ears, Rowdy. I said gem. G-E-M. You know, like a gemstone," said Patch.

"All right, I get it," said Rowdy. "It's the Texas blue topaz just like this one." He held up his right hand and showed a beautiful ring. "This here is what blue topaz looks like."

"Now, you're just showing off," said Patch. "Justin, when was the Battle of the Alamo?"

Justin scratched his head. "I always get it confused with Texas Independence Day. I think it is March 2, 1836, and Texas Independence Day is March 6. No, wait. It's the other way around. The Battle of the Alamo was on March 6, 1836. Final answer."

"You're right!" said Patch. "You had me scared there for a minute, cowboy. Dallas, it's your turn. Where was the final battle of the Texas Revolution?"

"The final battle was in San Jacinto, and it was on April 21, 1836. That's when General Santa Anna and his army were defeated," said Dallas.

"Good answer, Dallas," said Patch. "You boys have had some excellent teachers! Okay, Hank, it's your final turn. How do I know which way is up on the Texas flag?"

"My teacher told us how to remember the answer to that," said Hank. "The white stripe goes on the top and the red stripe is on the bottom. The way to remember it is to think about a cherry pie. The red cherries are on the bottom of the pie, and the whipped cream is on the top of it."

"Exactly!" said Patch. "Well, you cowboys did great on your Texas Trivia. Slim, do you have anything I could give these boys as a reward?"

"I've got some homemade ice cream left over from supper. Let me go git 'em a big bowl," said Slim. "I'll be right back."

As Slim headed toward the bunkhouse, Justin decided he needed to tell Rowdy and Patch how much he and his brothers had enjoyed being at the Double A. "Rowdy, we wanted to tell you and Patch how much we enjoyed our two weeks here on the ranch. Thank you for helping us have a good time."

"You're welcome," said Rowdy. "Shucks, I don't think we did anything special. We just put you to work and tried to keep you out of trouble."

"You and Patch taught us a lot about ranching, mending fences, and about Texas history," said Dallas.

"You helped us buy the dog and cat food for the animal shelter," said Hank.

"And, you helped us bring Miss Kitty home," said Dallas.

Slim returned with a tray loaded with bowls of homemade vanilla ice cream with a spoonful of beautiful red strawberries that he had picked himself at Fall Creek Farms. The boys picked out a bowl and began eating.

"Yum, this is delicious," said Justin. "Thank you, Slim."

"What is this?" asked Slim. "Well, I don't know where this came from. It looks like somebody put this envelope on my tray. Dallas, your eyes are better than mine. What is this?"

Dallas took the envelope and opened it up. He looked at what was inside, looked up at Slim, and said, "These are tickets to Fossil Rim! Three of them! Where did these come from?"

Rowdy explained, "Patch, Slim, and I decided to buy you boys some tickets to Fossil Rim to pay you for helping us out this summer.

Since you gave your money from the barn sale to the animal shelter, we decided to help you git that trip to Fossil Rim by gittin' those tickets for you. That means you'll have to come back so you can git out there and see all those wild animals."

"These are great!" said Dallas. They had never expected anything for working on the Double A.

"What about Jennie?" asked Hank.

"Her ticket is right here," said Rowdy. He pulled it out of his front shirt pocket. "I thought you might like to give it to her tomorrow before you head back to the city."

"Yes, sir," said Hank. "I'd like that."

The boys heard Ace whistle. He was standing on the front porch with their dad. He motioned with his arm for the boys to come on in.

The boys gave Rowdy a big hug to tell him good-bye. Rowdy said, "Let's do this like a man. Give me your hand, and let's shake." Justin held out his hand and shook Rowdy's hand. "That's not a handshake. That's more like a wet noodle. Firm up that hand, and give me a handshake with a good manly grip."

Justin gripped Rowdy's hand and gave him a firm handshake. "That's much better, Justin," said Rowdy. "Now, give these other cowboys a good handshake."

As Justin went around the campfire and shook hands with the cowboys, Dallas and Hank followed along behind and did the same thing. When they were through, the boys tipped their hats and said good-bye.

"Happy trails, cowboys," said Rowdy.

They walked back to the Main House with their heads hanging lower than usual. They were not ready to leave the Double A and their cowboy friends, but they knew they didn't have a choice. They would get up the next morning, pack their bags, and head back to the city.

CHAPTER 25
The Cat is Out of the Bag

MORNING CAME TOO SOON on the Double A Ranch for Justin, Dallas, and Hank. They packed their bags and set them by the front door before they headed to the kitchen table for breakfast. Ms. Adaline fixed their favorite breakfast consisting of scrambled eggs, bacon, biscuits, and gravy.

The boys' dad joined them at the table. "Good morning, boys," he said.

"Morning," said Justin. "I don't think I can say it's a 'good' morning."

The boys' mom slipped in at the table after pouring herself a cup of coffee. "Well, have you told them yet?" she asked.

"Told us what?" asked Justin.

"Your mom and I have something to tell you," their dad said. "We have been talking about selling our house and moving out of the city."

Their mom started smiling at them. "And, we decided that we would like to live closer to Ace and Ms. Adaline," she said.

The boys started smiling from ear to ear! They certainly liked that idea!

"There is a ranch for sale right down the road from here," their dad continued. "We've looked at it, and it looks like we will be moving back to Hood County and living right down the road!"

"What?" asked Hank. "We're moving to Hood County? All of us?"

"Yes," said his dad, "all of us. I'm going to begin looking for a job in Granbury, but until I find one, I'll be working here with Rowdy."

All three of the boys jumped up from the table and let out a loud "Yippee!" as they did their now famous happy dance all around the kitchen. Ms. Adaline even joined in as they danced around her. The boys' parents laughed and laughed at their excitement.

"Can I have a horse?" asked Hank.

"Do we have any barns on our ranch?" asked Dallas.

"Can we go look at it?" asked Justin.

"My, my," said their dad. "You sure have a lot of questions. Yes, you can have a horse. Yes, the ranch has some barns on it, and yes, I think we should load up right after Cowboy Church and go look at it."

The boys had forgotten it was Sunday. Rowdy would be starting the services for the cowboys soon. The boys grabbed their hats and took off running for the bunkhouse. They could hardly wait to tell Rowdy and Patch they were going to be moving right down the road.

"We'll see you at the bunkhouse," said Justin. "We've got to tell Rowdy and Patch the good news."

The boys made a flying jump onto the porch of the bunkhouse and dusted off their boots. Justin opened the door for his brothers, and they all went in together. They saw Rowdy as he talked with Patch and headed straight toward them.

"Good morning, boys," said Rowdy.

"Yes, sir," said Justin, "It is a good morning."

"No, it's not," said Dallas. "It's a *great* morning."

"It is?" asked Patch. "What's got you so happy, cowboy?"

"Dad bought a ranch right down the road, and we're moving to Hood County!" said Hank with all the excitement he could muster.

"Well, I'm glad that cat is out of the bag," said Rowdy. "I've had to bite my tongue several times this week so I wouldn't spoil their surprise. It looks like we're going to be neighbors!" Rowdy and Patch held out their hands to shake hands with the boys.

Ace, Ms. Adaline, and the boys' parents opened the door to the bunkhouse and joined the others who were ready to start Cowboy Church. The boys sat close to their parents at one end of a long table.

After Slim had led a couple of songs, Patch got up to speak. He said, "When I was in the hospital last week, I had more time on my hands than I ever have. I've always loved hearing good cowboy poetry like those that Red Steagall writes, but I have never tried writing any of it on my own. Until now, that is.

"Before I recite it, I want you to know that I think it's important that we old cowboys be a good example to the young cowboys like Justin, Dallas, and Hank. When I thought about it more, this here poem came to my head. I'll do my best to recite it from memory. Here goes:

Boys Become Men

Around the campfire at the end of the day
The cowboys gather to think back on the way
The cattle were worked and fences were mended, and
The hands worked hard just the way God intended.
The campfire's now burnin' with flames of white heat
And cowboys are jawin' with tales hard to beat.
The stories they tell to the new bunch of hands
Will be told and retold 'cause it's part of the plan
To train up the kids we hired on to teach
And pass down traditions we hope they don't breach.
Those youngin's are watchin' the hands of today
And picturin' themselves as ranchers one day.
Boys become men, and the men they're now watchin'
Will hand over the reins when the young men start ranchin.'"

Patch looked down at the floor for a moment, and then continued, "Now, I know Red Steagall's not gonna give that poem a prize, but I wanted to share it with all of you. More than ever I realize that sometime or another I'm gonna have to hang up my spurs one last time. Since I don't have any youngin's of my own, I kinda feel like those three boys over there are the closest I'll ever git to having sons." He pointed to Justin, Dallas, and Hank as he spoke. "Boys, I want you to know that I'll do my best to show you the right way to ranch and the right way to live. I ain't perfect, you know, but I'll do my best to teach you how to become the cowboys you were born to be.

"I heard this morning that those boys are going to be moving into our neck of the woods real soon. I think I'm just as excited about that as they are," continued Patch. He looked over at the boys, and said, "Now, when Rowdy starts gettin' too ornery, I can just slip over to your place!"

Rowdy smiled and shook his head. "Thanks for givin' me a heads-up on where your hidey-hole is going to be, Patch." Everyone laughed, and Patch gave them one of his big smiles showing lots of empty spaces as he found a seat at the table. After Rowdy said a few words, the service was over.

Another summer at the Double A Ranch was over for the boys. Life was getting ready to change for all of them. The boys would be living in a new house on a new ranch, going to a new school, and making new friends. They would be leaving those pastures of concrete and asphalt in the rear-view mirror for some pastures made of fresh green grass and cool flowing creeks.

After a stop at the Dilka Ranch to give Jennie her ticket to Fossil Rim and to tell her the good news, the boys got to see the ranch they would soon be calling home. It was about five miles down the road and on the other side of the Dilka Ranch. They were ready to become real cowboys now, not just city slickers. They would become the next generation of cowboys and be just like the cowboys they admired the most: Ace, Rowdy, Patch, and their dad.

The wind began to blow. The tree tops swayed gently with the afternoon breeze. Justin and Hank began kicking up the dirt and looking for arrowheads and treasures on their new ranch. Dallas watched them as he climbed up onto a big white rock, sat down, and looked out across the land. He began to daydream, and he thought for a moment he could hear Rowdy calling out in the wind, "Happy trails, cowboys!" He smiled. He knew he was going to have many happy days of adventures, campfires, and cowboy tales ahead of him. He couldn't wait to see where those happy trails would lead him and his brothers.

Fact and Fiction

Chapter 1 – The characters of Justin, Dallas, Hank, their parents, Ace, and Ms. Adaline are characters created by the author. The Double A Ranch in Hood County, Texas, is fictitious as far as the author knows.

Chapter 4 – Rowdy and Patch are fictitious characters.

Chapter 5 – It is true that the Comanche lived in Hood County and used Comanche Peak as a lookout and a meeting place. The town of Lipan in Hood County was named after a tribe of Apache.

Chapter 6 – It is true that at one time Caddo, Comanche, and Lipan Apache lived in the Hood County area along with the Tonkawa, Kiowa, and Wichita. They were driven off their lands when the Anglo settlers uprooted them in order to claim land and wild game for their personal use in the 1850s. David Crockett was a hero at the Battle of the Alamo. The facts about him are true. His wife, Elizabeth, was really given land in present day Hood County. The facts given about her and her family are correct. Ken Hendricks is a real person and is the great-great grandson of David and Elizabeth Crockett. He and his wife, Jessie, are long-time residents of Hood County. Elizabeth Crockett is buried in the historical Acton Cemetery.

Chapter 7 – Jennie is a fictitious character although she is based on a real person, Kellie Dilka Lambert, Miss Rodeo America, 1988, who is currently an educator in Granbury, Texas.

Chapter 8 – The information on the empresario and Father of Texas Stephen F. Austin is true. Sam Houston was the first President of the Republic of Texas.

Chapter 9 – The Dinosaur State Park (www.tpwd.state.tx.us/state-parks/dinosaur-valley) and Dinosaur World (www.tpwd.state.tx.us/state-parks/dinosaur-valley) are located just outside of Glen Rose, Texas, in Somervell County. The information on horned frogs is true. The Dust Bowl actually occurred in the 1930s due to drought, extended periods of high wind, and a failure to use dry farming methods to prevent wind erosion.

Chapter 10 – The information about Captain Richard King and the King Ranch is true. Charles Goodnight, Oliver Loving, Bose Ikard, John Simpson Chisum, and Jesse Chisholm were real cowboys who played a major role in the cattle ranching industry in early Texas and the southwestern part of the U. S. The information presented in this chapter about them is true. Squaw Creek is a real lake located next to the nuclear plant in Somervell County. It was closed after September 11, 2001, for security measures.

Chapter 12 – It is true that Texas Christian University (TCU) had its beginnings in Hood County, Texas, as Add-Ran College. The historical information presented about the university is correct.

Chapter 14 – The information presented in this chapter about Hood County, the old Hood County jail, Jesse F. and Jacob Nutt, the Nutt House, and Mary Lou Watkins is true. The legends of John Wilkes Booth and Jesse James are told as fact in Hood County, but they are based on conflicting historical information. It has not been resolved at this time whether the Granbury legends are true or not, and will probably always be considered legends. Rinky Tinks was a popular ice cream parlor in Granbury for many years. The last owners of Rinky Tinks were Bob and Jo Ann Skelton. Bobby Skel was the recording name for Bob Skelton. He was a musician and recording artist in the 1960s.

Chapter 15 – The Dilka Ranch is not located in Hood County, Texas. Fossil Rim Wildlife Center (www.fossilrim.org) is actually located just west of Glen Rose, Texas, in Somervell County, and is a popular visitor attraction.

Chapter 17 – The character of Nurse Lucas is fictional. However, she is named after a real nurse, Rebecca Lucas, from Lake Granbury Medical Center in Granbury.

Chapter 18 – Lizzie Johnson was a real cattle baroness who moved to Texas from Missouri in 1844 with her family. Her real name was Elizabeth Ellen "Lizzie" Johnson Williams. She married Hezekiah Williams in 1879, at the age of 39. The information presented about her is true. She is buried in the Oakwood Cemetery in Austin, Texas.

Chapter 22 – There is an animal shelter in Acton, Texas, that is a rescue facility for dogs and cats. Donations are accepted and appreciated. Dixie is a fictitious character named after Dixie Lee Hedgecock of Granbury, TX, an employee of Lake Granbury Medical Center.

Chapter 23 – "Texas, Our Texas" is the Texas State Song. It was written in 1924 by William John and Gladys Yoakum Wright Marsh. Mr. Marsh came to Texas as a young man from England. Gladys was a resident of Fort Worth. Mr. Marsh is buried in the Greenwood Memorial Park, in Fort Worth, Texas. His wife, Gladys, is buried in McKinney, Texas, in the Pecan Grove Cemetery.

Chapter 24 – The trivia game facts are true. Fall Creek Farms (upicktx.com) is actually located on Fall Creek Highway in the southeastern part of Hood County, Texas. They raise strawberries and peaches. When harvest time arrives, people may come out and pick their own fresh fruit. The poem, *Boys Become Men,* was written by the author, Nancy Sifford Alana. Red Steagall is a real cowboy poet, songwriter, and storyteller (redsteagall.com).

Ms. Adaline's Sauerkraut Cake

2/3 cup butter or margarine
1 ½ cups of sugar
3 eggs
1 t. vanilla
½ cup cocoa
2 ¼ cups flour
1 t. baking powder
1 t. baking soda
¼ t. salt
1 cup water
2/3 cup well-rinsed, drained, and chopped sauerkraut

Preheat oven to 350 degrees. Prepare your baking pan/pans by greasing with butter or margarine. Cream butter and sugar together. Beat in eggs and vanilla. Sift dry ingredients together. Add alternately with water to egg mixture. Stir in kraut. Bake at 350 degrees about 30-40 minutes or tests done with a dry straw when inserted into the cake. Frost with your favorite chocolate icing. The sauerkraut cannot be tasted and adds moisture to the cake. This recipe was from the recipe box of Margaret Whitt Sifford of Lubbock, TX.

Mrs. Meek's Pecan Pie

1 cup sugar
¼ tsp. salt
3 eggs
3 Tbsp. butter, melted
1 cup of white Karo syrup
1 tsp. vanilla
1 cup pecans, broken
1 9-inch pie shell

Preheat oven to 450 degrees. (Turn down to 350 degrees when you put pie in the oven.) Stir together sugar, salt, and eggs gently. Do not whip. Add melted butter, Karo, vanilla, and pecans. Stir.

Pour into unbaked pie shell. Bake for 1 hour.

It is deeee-licious!

Ms. Adaline's Chicken and Dumplings

1 Chicken, whole
3 Chicken bouillon cubes
1/4 cup butter or margarine
1/2 tsp. salt
1/2 tsp. baking powder
1 c. flour
1 egg
1 pt. milk or half and half
Salt and pepper to taste

Cook chicken in boiling salted water until tender. Remove chicken from broth; cool. Remove chicken from bones; return chicken to broth and add the bouillon cubes. Keep warm.

Mix butter, salt, baking powder, and flour until mixture resembles meal. Add egg and enough ice water to make a stiff dough. Roll out on floured surface as thin as possible; cut into strips. Heat the milk; do not boil. Stir milk into chicken broth and chicken; season with salt and pepper. Bring to a boil; add dumplings, one at a time. Cook for about 15 minutes or until dumplings are done. This recipe is one of the author's favorites.

Sources

Aaron Nelsen, "Where the Santa Gertrudis Roam," *Texas Highways*, November, 2013.

Bose Ikard. Find A Grave. Accessed September, 2013. findagrave.com.

Jesse Chisholm-Peacemaker of the Plains. Accessed September, 2013 from http://www.electricscotland.com.

John Ashton and Edgar P. Sneed. King Ranch. Accessed September, 2013. www.tshaonline.org/handbook.

Kathy Weiser. Legends of America. January, 2008. Accessed September, 2013. www.legendsofamerica.com/we-goodnight-lovingtrail.html.

Kellie Dilka Lambert. Personal Interview by Nancy Alana. 2013.

Kenneth Hendricks. Personal Interview by Nancy Alana. 2013.

Larry L. Smith, "ARMADILLO," *Handbook of Texas Online* (www.tshaonline.org/handbook/online/articles/tca02), Accessed September, 2013. Published by the Texas State Historical Association.

Lizzie Johnson (Williams). Great Texas Women. Accessed September, 2013. www.utexas.edu/gtw/johnson_.williams.php.

Mary Estelle Gott Saltarelli. *Historic Hood County, An Illustrated History*. 2009. San Antonio, TX. Historical Publishing Network.

Ralph W. Steen, "TEXAS DECLARATION OF INDEPENDENCE," *Handbook of Texas Online* (www.tshaonline.org/handbook/online/articles/mjtce), Accessed September, 2013. Published by the Texas State Historical Association.

The Legacy. King Ranch. Accessed September, 2013 from king-ranch.com

Universe Magic. The Horned Lizard: Blood Squirting Lizard. Accessed September, 2013. www.universemagic.com.

8655265R00115

Made in the USA
San Bernardino, CA
19 February 2014